Vanishing Herds

T0329286

H.R. Ole Kulet

sasa
sema

an imprint of

LONGHORN

PUBLISHERS
expanding minds

Published by Sasa Sema Publications
An imprint of Longhorn Publishers

Longhorn Kenya Ltd.,
Funzi Road, Industrial Area,
P.O. Box 18033-00500,
Nairobi, Kenya.

Longhorn Publishers (U) Ltd.,
Plot 731, Kamwokya Area,
Mawanda Road, P.O. Box 24745,
Kampala, Uganda.

Longhorn Publishers (Tanzania) Ltd.,
Kinondoni, Plot No. 4 Block 37B,
Kawawa Road,
P.O. Box 1237,
Dar es Salaam, Tanzania.

First published 2011

Cover Illustration and design by Tuf Mulokwa

ISBN 998 9966 361 144 8

Printed by English Press Ltd.,
off Enterprise Road, Industrial Area,
P.O. Box 30127-00100,
Nairobi, Kenya.

Dedication

This book is dedicated to my beloved daughter, Eddah Sein, from whom I borrowed the name of one of the characters, the respected environmentalist.

The book is also dedicated to all environmentalists who struggle tirelessly to ensure that the degraded environment and decimated forests are restored. I salute and applaud the KWS and KEFRI for restoring animal habitats and conserving water towers.

CHAPTER 1

When Norpisia and Kedoki stepped out of Eddah Sein's house in Nakuru town, they did not know how much their story had stirred the minds of the people who had read it. They did not know that Norpisia had become a heroine and a celebrity. Anything associated with her name had become sensational owing to the prominence given by the daily newspapers which highlighted her tragedy when she nearly lost her life in that freakish flood. She and her husband lost all their livestock. They also lost her four tamed wildebeests that had become a tourist attraction during the famous annual event when migratory herds of wild animals crossed Enkipai river on their way to the southern grasslands.

Kedoki thought their presence in Nakuru town would give him an opportunity to show his wife, who had never been to Nakuru before, what he knew of the town. He did not know much about it. He had seen it only once, thirty years earlier when, as a young boy in the company of his father and other pastoralists, he drove their herd of cattle through the then small town. What he could still remember vaguely about the town, was its dusty streets, scattered wood and corrugated iron sheet godowns and a long line of shabby Indian *dukas*.

He recalled seeing a narrow single-track railway line on which a hooting steam-spewing locomotive hurtled down from the Mau escarpment pulling along with what appeared to him then, like many oblong blocks. Neither he and the other boys, nor their cattle had before seen such a strange, smoke-billowing monster. When it hooted, they all panicked and ran with fright down toward Lake Nakuru. They disappeared into the thick bushes around the lake. It took the old men the whole afternoon to round them up and re-assure the boys that the monster was not a vampire out to devour them.

So, on that beautiful sunny morning when the couple was told they were going to meet a high ranking officer in the environment conservation office, Norpisia put on her new colourful *lesos* and adorned herself with a beautiful multi-coloured bead necklace. She wore the white rubber shoes that Sein, the respected environmentalist, had brought. Kedoki on the other hand, wore his red *shukas* on top of which he put on his Enkila-oo-ndeerri, a beautiful outer garment made from soft wooly hyrax skins sewn into a gown-like cloak. In his hands, he carried a black knobkerrie and a fly-whisk. The handle was beautifully decorated with multi-coloured beads.

People cheered wildly when they saw the couple emerge from Sein's house. Some whispered among themselves wondering whether the woman in their presence was capable of doing what had been reported in the papers. If it was true that she had spearheaded groups of women to plant thousands of trees that helped to resuscitate the degraded environment, then, she was the people's heroine.

Newspaper pictures of large forest covers with lines of healthy green trees, that were said to have been planted through her efforts, awed those who saw them. And the rains that had returned in earnest, were partly attributed to the trees she, and others that she influenced, had planted.

As Norpisia and Kedoki got into Sein's Suzuki vehicle, they were already mesmerized by the attention they were attracting. Those who recognized them waved cheerfully and hooted when they saw them pass. Soon, they were at the centre of Nakuru town. Although he expected to see many new buildings, Kedoki's mind was not prepared for what lay before their eyes. The town was unrecognizable to him and the spectacular view was beyond his wildest imagination. He noted with amazement that the town was neatly lined with multi-storied buildings. Plate-glass shop-fronts lined the wide tarmacked streets, while modern hotels, restaurants and offices were systematically located, most likely, in accordance with laid down plans. Bougainvillea blossoms blazed on perimeter walls of some buildings. On one end of the streets, was a grove of giant jacaranda trees. Norpisia who had not seen the town before, was entranced. But what surprised and nearly frightened them, was the number of people in the streets. Multitudes of people walked up and down with as much determination as red ants. Equally scaring to the nomadic couple, was the number of vehicles, motor-bikes and bicycles which cruised up and down the busy streets.

The Suzuki briefly slowed down at a traffic snarl-up on Mburu Gichua Road. At that hour of the day, the street was crowded and bustling with market women carrying basketfuls of vegetables and fruits, tradesmen walking briskly following porters who meandered through crowds carrying heavy loads on their shoulders; and hordes of hawkers touting for business. Soon, they turned and took Oginga Odinga road, past Shades and Taidys hotels; then crossed the last intersections. Sein saw the sign-board ahead indicating that they were close to the office of the officer in charge of environmental matters. She slowed down, to calm her nerves.

As she drove the last few metres to their destination, Sein gave thought to the couple she was driving in her vehicle. Although Norpisia had become a celebrity after the dailies made public her tireless efforts in resuscitating the environment, they had also exposed the tragic side of her life when the earlier devastating drought decimated their herd, reducing it from one thousand heads to a mere one hundred. Ironically, after helping to plant thousands of trees, she was unfortunate to have fallen victim of the resultant floods that nearly claimed her life. The floods impoverished them further by drowning their last one hundred heads of cattle, leaving them helpless and destitute. Despite that drawback, Norpisia was still optimistic that if they only got a single cow, they

4

would be able to re-establish their life. However, Sein was rather realistic. Although she managed to convince the governor that Norpisia deserved nomination for an award in recognition of her effort, nobody else thought along these lines. As matters stood, Norpisia had no house, no cattle, and no food to give to her child. In these circumstances, Sein imagined the representative of the governor standing on the podium, handing a shiny medal to Norpisia. Amidst applause and clapping of hands, she imagined Norpisia receiving the shiny piece of round metal, and wondering whether she could sell it to buy herself some food.

By the time they got to their destination, Sein's mind was already troubled. She saw all things in their extremity: the haves and the have nots, the oppressed and the oppressors, the big and the small and the old and the young. So, when she parked her small ancient Suzuki into the parking bay of the imposing office complex, she couldn't help but compare her Suzuki with the sleek cars parked on either side. The Suzuki stood awkwardly beside the huge shining Benz belonging to the representative of the governor. Sein, who did not ordinarily think of cars as status symbols found herself peering at the luxurious vehicle with a critical eye.

Looking at it as it stood in grandeur beside her dusty Suzuki, a curious feeling pervaded her mind. Oddly, she perceived that cars had their own peculiar character and personality. Sein concluded that the Benz was clearly satisfied with itself, that it was almost preening itself, like an overfed lion basking in the sun. And her small battered car was praying that its owner would one day have mercy, strength and resources to overhaul its engine, to resuscitate it and give it a new lease of life! It had traversed and crisscrossed the countryside as they sensitized people on the need to conserve the environment, and it clearly required a fresh coat of paint.

The representative of the governor eventually emerged from his office to a planned procession heading to the stadium. In front was a brass-band that played what Norpisia thought was mind-soothing music. They walked side by side with Sein and others who were to be awarded medals that afternoon. They walked swiftly down the road that led to the stadium, a wide street that was partly lined with shops, a few churches and mosques, and some residential houses. While Kedoki found that part of town impressive, Norpisia thought it utterly formless and sordid. Having recently come from a countryside boasting of rehabilitated forests where people lived in a hale and hearty atmosphere, she shrank uncomfortably from the amorphous gritty street. She felt cruelly exposed to every stare as they passed through what she considered to be a stretch of torment. It seemed strange that after the physical and mental torment she underwent when she nearly drowned in the flooded Ilkarian river, she still submitted to the insufferable torture of participating in a meaningless procession that snaked between rows of staring masses. It was as if she was suffocating like an Olobel-kik, the dung-beetle, frolicking in dung. She was filled with repulsion.

6

The procession headed toward the stadium led by the brass-band. Norpisia followed, half-dazed as if she was treading on the air. Her heart contracted and she felt dizzy.

At the stadium entrance stood a multitude of excited people, waiting to see the famous woman pastoralist. She was said to have miraculously changed an arid and desolate wasteland into a garden of Eden. Even as the people applauded her, Norpisia's xenophobic feelings, which she thought she had overcome, returned to haunt her. Her heart cried out within her, as if it was in the midst of a terrible ordeal.

"I don't want to go any farther," Norpisia told Sein weakly as she suddenly stopped. And turning to her husband as if asking for protection, she said to him petulantly, "Look at all these people staring at us!"

"Never mind them," Sein whispered reassuringly. "They mean no harm at all."

"In fact, they admire and respect you," added Kedoki trying to cheer up his wife.

"But must we go through this throng of people?" asked Norpisia anxiously "Is there no other way to get there?"

Without answering her, Sein got hold of Norpisia's hand and steered her through the crowd to the stand that had been reserved for the recipients of awards. Kedoki sat next to them near the podium.

At three o'clock, the dignitaries began to arrive. There was an excited stir in the crowd as the shiny black

Benz drove in. Soon, the representative of the governor, his entourage and other guests, mounted the steps and walked on the red carpet to the podium.

Norpisia sat in silence between her husband and Eddah Sein, her face averted. She regretted her acceptance to participate in that charade, where she had to face all those people in the stadium as if she were on trial. She shuddered with nervous apprehension and her body convulsed with agitation.

When the representative of the governor stood up to speak, he profusely praised Norpisia for her unprecedented accomplishment in the resuscitation, rehabilitation and the conservation of the environment. He described as unsurpassed, her organizational skills and leadership qualities that enabled her marshal groups of women to plant thousands of tree-seedlings that matured into invaluable forests. He paid tribute to similar projects that had been replicated all over the country.

He revealed that those who had grabbed forest land and cut down trees have since appreciated the positive results of a rehabilitated environment that had helped reverse the adverse effects of drought and stabilized weather patterns. As a result, they had vacated such lands and returned them to government for re-afforestation.

Finally, he challenged the scribes to write down the history of the once degraded and now rehabilitated environment, noting that when that was done, Norpisia's name would rank high among those individuals who did a lot to bring back sobriety into a situation that had threatened to go out of control.

While the representative of the governor spoke, Kedoki's mind travelled back to Eorr-Narasha and to that incentive scheme that Sein had started. It was called; *Sheep for Trees Initiative* in which villagers were given a sheep for a fixed number of trees planted. If the scheme ever were to return, he whispered to himself, he would plant so many trees; to earn him enough sheep to restart his life again.

Kedoki's reverie was interrupted when Norpisia was called forward to receive her award. Upon hearing her name, Norpisia panicked. A terrible storm came over her and she felt as if she was drowning. She was possessed by devastating hopelessness. Never before had she known such pang of utter helplessness. As she involuntarily approached the podium, she suddenly collapsed, prompting Sein and Kedoki to rush forward, lift her up and carry her away.

CHAPTER 2

It had been four years since then but the memory of that atrocious and frightful day was still vividly fresh in Norpisia's mind. It was late in the evening after her mother had finished milking and began preparing their evening meal when the hideous men struck, shooting at the fleeing villagers indiscriminately, while herding off the livestock. She was about fourteen years then and could still recall her family fleeing. Her mother running, holding the hand of her youngest brother who was about ten years old at that time. Her older siblings, a brother and a sister, ran faster than the rest. They disappeared into the bushes while she ran after her mother fearfully tugging at her *shukas*. Her father, Messopirr, who limbed badly from an earlier injury caused by the same bandits, hobbled behind everyone else holding his spear, ready to defend them when it became necessary.

Norpisia recalled how chilling the atmosphere became especially when the crack sound of gun fire exploded in their ears. The horrendous sound had sent everyone hurtling into the bushes as the evening turned from dusk into darkness. None followed the other as they scattered in all directions.

It was early the following morning when they regrouped that the ghastly reality hit them. They sorrowfully learnt that Norpisia's elder brother and sister had been shot dead by bandits that night. They all grieved without restraint. Norpisia's mother was inconsolable.

They later gathered in their home to mourn the death of their beloved ones. Neighbours and friends came to console them. Among those who came was a man Norpisia had not seen before. Although the atmosphere was permeated with sorrow from what had happened, Norpisia thought the man appeared more sorrowful than everybody else. She was very sorry for him when she later learnt that he too had lost a brother and a sister to the beastly bandits that same night. She considered him strong-hearted for him to commiserate with them when he had funeral arrangements to attend to at his home. Filled with pity for the man, Norpisia observed him more closely. He was a quiet, tall and well-built man of about thirty. He wore bright red *shukas* underneath a black and red checked blanket. She identified a determined silent demeanour that she attributed to his great loss.

Norpisia did not see the man soon after this meeting. Her parents, determined to help her cope with the pain of losing her siblings, dispatched her to the farthest end of Olomuruti to the home of her grandmother. Her father felt she was safer there from the frequent bandit attacks.

After Norpisia had relocated, the man whose name she learnt later was Kedoki, continued to visit her parents.

Unknown to Norpisia, Kedoki had proposed to marry her. The brewed engagement mead was drank by elders while the *enkaputi* negotiations were entered into and finalized. Without being consulted, Norpisia was given for marriage to Kedoki.

That should not have worried Norpisia. At eighteen years, she knew she was no longer an *entiapederoi* – a tomboy – but a marriageable girl who should have been ready for initiation any time a suitor came calling. Although she had known that she would inevitably get married soon, she always wondered what kind of man would approach her father wanting to marry her. Her hope had always been that a man from the neighbourhood would engage her for she dreaded leaving her family for a strange place.

Norpisia learnt a lot of things during the four years that she lived with her grandmother. Being an *enkoiboni*, her grandmother was a renown medicine woman who was reputed to possess supernatural powers. She, therefore, taught Norpisia the art of clairvoyance, divination and incantation. As a medicine woman, she was an expert in mixing and preparation of herbal medicine. Many times, she took Norpisia with her into the forest where she exposed her to various types of roots, barks, berries and nuts from which she derived her medicinal preparations. This, she concocted into potent curatives. She used them to treat all kinds of illnesses. When her patients came for treatment, she made Norpisia sit through the treatments so that she could learn how to treat and nurse the sick. After sometime, her grandmother began to allow her to treat minor ailments and to mix concoctions that she tested before she administered them to patients.

Besides learning herbal medicine and other domestic chores, Norpisia was taught self-defence and self-reliance skills by her male relatives who lived with her grandmother. She mastered the use of such weapons as spears, bows and arrows, knives and knobkerries, to the extent that she could wield them as expertly as any man would. She also learnt animal husbandry. She was also taught to appreciate her role as a woman, wife and a potential mother.

Norpisia knew something was afoot when Messopirr sent her brother to fetch her from her grandmother's home. When they arrived, they were informed that the family was in the nearby forest, where her father had slaughtered a ram for them. She followed her brother to the hide-out in the dense forest where her father often retreated when he was in need of privacy or when he wanted to slaughter a sheep exclusively for his family. The moment she walked into the forest, Norpisia knew clairvoyantly that her father had not called her to enjoy a bite of mutton.

It took a few moments for her eyes to adjust to the dim light in the silent forest. She immediately felt the cool damp air and smelled the rich, humid foliage. Blended with the smell of foliage that was carried to her nostrils by the breeze was the appetizing aroma of roast meat. As

Norpisia got closer, the smells became stronger and got mixed with the familiar smell of wood smoke.

The moment her eyes adjusted to the dim light, Norpisia furtively glanced at a man seated next to her father. On recognizing him, she quickly looked away, her heart palpitating. For some unknown reasons, she thought the man's presence could have been the reason her father had summoned her. She approached her father, bowed to greet him, and went to where her mother was seated and hugged her, kissing her lightly on her lips. She did not know how to react to the presence of the stranger. Her father with a wave of his hand uttered a terse order, asking her to bring a calabash of water to the man. As Norpisia walked away, her father turned and said something to the man. The man looked at Norpisia as she crossed the small clearing where they were seated, carrying the calabash of water in her hands. And as she handed the calabash to him, their eyes met. She quickly looked away as the man fixed his stare at her.

"Ne yeiyo-ai nanyorr," Messopirr called her fondly.

"Yeo," Norpisia answered, her heart throbbing anxiously, her eyes down cast.

"Get to know this man here," he told her. "Soon, you will be seeing him more frequently. His name is Kedoki. If you remember, he is the man who lost a brother and a sister at the same time you lost your siblings."

Her mouth suddenly went dry and she licked her lips nervously. She was not prepared for the sudden announcement. But she knew that at eighteen, she ought to have been a wife. It was not the norm for a girl of her

14

age to be still living in her father's homestead.

"I do remember him," she said demurely.

Nothing more was said about the matter. After they had eaten, they reclined against tree trunks and relaxed. From time to time, Norpisia furtively stole a glance at her father and the man who, although still a stranger, was now somehow linked with her. She tried to eavesdrop on their conversation, but they kept their voices low as was the norm while in the forest. This was necessary so as to listen for other sounds that might signal danger. Occasionally, when she could make out a few words of what they were saying, Norpisia was relieved to hear that their conversation was not about her. They were discussing the man's herd of cattle which, from their talk, was very large. In addition to owning more than a thousand heads of cattle, he also owned a flock of three hundred sheep, three hundred goats and tens of donkeys. He also owned several dogs. Having lost his brother and sister to the brutal bandits, the man was saying he did not know what to do. He longed to go back to his home at Nkararo in Olorukoti, but was unable to do so, for he could not drive the large herd alone, nor could he manage to protect it from predators and cattle rustlers.

What Norpisia did not know at that time was that the betrothal negotiations had long been concluded and *enkaputi* confirmed. She learnt later that the sole purpose for that day's meeting was simply to give the man an opportunity to have a good look at his would-be bride and get to know her better.

At first, Messopirr was reluctant to discuss his daughter's marriage proposed with a stranger. So, he only accepted the man as a guest in his home and whenever he visited them, he limited their conversation to matters about cattle, sheep, and goats. However, he neither accepted nor rejected him as a potential son-in-law. He left the matter in abeyance as he studied him.

For the next three years, Kedoki continued to pester Messopirr asking that he be allowed to marry her. He literally begged him to enter into betrothal negotiations with the family. Finally, his persistence won him acceptance. However, something else also hastened the softening of Messopirr's hardline stand. Ever since his two children died in the brutal hands of bandits, Norpisia's father had not stopped thinking of the safety of his surviving daughter. Recently, he had the scare of his life when the beastly bandits struck a village close to Norpisia's grandmother's home, where he had sent his daughter. He now had to re-think not only her immediate, but her long term safety and future. He thus gave Kedoki's proposal to marry Norpisia, a second thought. Since Kedoki proposed to marry her and take her to Nkararo in Olorukoti, far from Olomuruti, Messopirr considered that the answer to his daughter's safety. It would give her a secure future.

Once the door to negotiations was opened, nothing held back the process again and all matters were candidly discussed and speedily concluded. The requisite bride-price was paid, the initiation day agreed upon, and the day of marriage set.

From the moment Norpisia arrived, Kedoki had taken every opportunity to study her. He had only seen her once on that day of mourning when she accompanied other girls to the river to draw water.

When she arrived with her brother that afternoon, he noted that she had grown tall, a good match for his six feet frame. Her lithe wiry muscles were sharply defined in her long arms and legs. Before she went to live with her grandmother four years earlier, he recalled, she was small-bodied and looked somewhat weak. But now four years later, she had grown big and stronger.

The red *shukas* she wore, fitted her comfortably, but did not hide her firm, full breasts, or her womanly hips that curved back to her well-rounded body.

Her face was heart-shaped with high cheek-bones, a well-defined jaw and a smooth narrow chin. Her large brown eyes gleamed actively. Her nose was straight and finely made, and her smooth lips that curved up at the corners were momentarily opened and pulled back, exposing her white pearl-like teeth in a smile that lit up her eyes.

Six months after her initiation day, Norpisia's marriage day arrived. Women from Olomuruti village were all there to see her off, and so were a few elders. It was an unusual wedding that did not have a best man, otherwise known as *shepu-Ilkerra*. Practically being a simple wedding where the groom and the bride would immediately after the wedding embark on a long journey, it was agreed that there was no need for a best man.

So, on the wedding day, the rising sun peered over the east with a blinding burst of light. It illuminated Norpisia's father's homestead. To the west, in the direction the bridegroom and his bride would soon go, a flat, utterly featureless plain stretched out before them. Above it, the sky was a shade of blue so stunningly brilliant that it seemed to glow with its own light in a colour beyond description. Whether it was a reality or an illusion borne of the fact that she was sadly leaving behind all that she had known and loved, Norpisia did not know.

After they were blessed by elders, Kedoki and Norpisia started off across the plain, as husband and wife, on their long journey to Nkararo in Olorukoti.

CHAPTER 3

Kedoki planned to leave Olomuruti and begin his journey to Nkararo in Olorukoti early in the month before the onset of the rains. Having studied the weather patterns and known the seasons after observing them for several years, he knew that when the rain fell, as it always did later in that month, Enkare-Narok river would flood. It would be extremely hazardous to cross especially now that he had a lot of young stock in his herd.

For four years, he had been planning to leave but each time he had had to postpone the journey when he failed to receive a definite word from Messopirr, Norpisia's father, regarding his proposal to marry his daughter. Now he was ready to begin the journey. He was delighted that he had someone to assist him make weighty decisions. He was now wiser, and he paraphrased these wise words when he said: clever was the eye that ventured out. Although he was saddened that he would be travelling back to Nkararo without his departed siblings, victims of bandits attacks, he was consoled to know that he was taking back to his village, a herd of over one thousand heads of cattle, up from the four hundred that he had when he began his journey in pursuit of green pastures.

In addition, he had three hundred sheep and three hundred goats. Luck had smiled on him.

Kedoki hoped that his return to Nkararo, while driving the largest herd of cattle ever seen in the village, and presenting Norpisia to his parents and friends as the most beautiful woman that they had ever seen, would be a reason for jubilation. And no doubt, he believed he would be counted among the wealthiest men in Nkararo.

So, on the day Kedoki decided to begin the long journey, he was joined by Norpisia and together, they drove their herd out of their temporary homestead onto the plains. The animals raised up a cloud of dust that a gust of wind picked and swirled into the sky. Curious villagers came out of their homesteads to admire the many well-fed black and white cattle that moved in long windy columns, tinkling bells dangling from the necks of buffalo-like oxen, as they were driven further afield.

Kedoki ran up and down controlling the movement of the cattle, while Norpisia followed the herd from the rear, walking slowly, with a forlorn expression on her face. Occasionally, she thought of her grandmother, her mother, relatives and friends that she was leaving behind. She was overcome by anguish, broke down and wept. From time to time, in the course of rounding up the cattle, Kedoki came closer to where Norpisia was, he threw a furtive glance at her, wondering what to tell her to lift up her spirits. He knew that her heart was heavy; she was leaving behind all the people she had known and loved and she was now headed to an undisclosed destination with a husband she hardly knew. Given time, he reassured himself confidently, Norpisia would know that what awaited her was nothing but felicity.

Kedoki watched her from a distance. He thought Norpisia was behaving in a strange manner. He saw her stop and turn back to face the direction of Olomuruti, the village that they had left behind.

She held a slender, smoothly polished stick on which she leaned slightly, her face averted as she stared at the distant village. She stood in profile, her back and shoulders straight, the sun gleaming on her dark brown skin and the curves of her body standing out clearly under the *lesos* she wore. It was as if she was emotionally bidding farewell to the village in which she was born and bred, where all her memories were held and stored. Once she was done, she turned and faced the direction toward which they were going. She appeared to have lightened up. When she resumed her walk behind the herd, she carried out her duties wholeheartedly. When he later talked to her, he was happy to find her responding positively.

Later that day, as he drove the herd through a wooded area, it pleased him to see her take charge, walking up and down controlling the movement of the cattle so that they slowed down to graze between bushes. Kedoki would then stand before the herd whistling happily, occasionally shouting to turn back those animals that strayed.

In the evening, Kedoki informed Norpisia that he was

looking for a suitable place to set up camp for the night. He identified a strategic location near a small stream. Once she surveyed the spot and decided where she was going to put up her kitchen, Kedoki stood back and watched her keenly as she swung into action. Norpisia quickly rounded up the donkeys that carried their household effects and brought them to the campsite, off-loaded them and began to sort out the goods. She felt sad when it occurred to her that those very items, which included pots, mugs, calabashes and other essential tools, once belonged to Kedoki's sister who was killed by bandits. That reminded her of her departed siblings. Tears welled up in her eyes, but she blew her nose and went back to her chores.

She offloaded poles from one of the donkeys and erected them on the ground. Within no time, she had set up a temporary hut of sticks and hides called *olngoborr*. Then she took a panga and went out to fetch firewood.

As Norpisia busied herself with her domestic chores, Kedoki walked to the nearby thorn bushes, cut down branches and dragged them to the place where they had set up their camp. He erected a thorn fence and constructed a cattle enclosure. At sunset, he walked to the pastures and herded the flock into the enclosure. He dragged in more thorn branches to close the entrance.

That done, he proceeded to Norpisia's *olngoborr* and made preparations to kindle a fire. From his quiver, he pulled out a slender fire stick called *olpiron* and a flat plank of wood called *enoose*. He twirled the slender stick against the plank of wood until the friction sent a wisp of smoke into the air. He repeated the process until a tiny spark flew onto the leaves that he placed next to the plank of wood. He quickly cupped his hands around the tiny spark and blew gently. A small coal glowed with a red light and a small shower of tiny amber-colour sparks. A second gentle blow produced a small flame. He added twigs and small splinters of wood, and when the fire crackled cheerfully, he added firewood. By the time Norpisia came in with more firewood, a roaring fire was burning brightly outside the *olngoborr*.

As darkness crept in the camp, Norpisia completed milking and left the cattle enclosure. She got back to the *olngoborr*, took out a tin that contained meat preserved in sheep fat called *olpurda* and served supper. They both sat down to chew the meat, each one of them keeping their thoughts to themselves.

Kedoki tossed more firewood onto the fire, as darkness fell. The cool breeze that blew from the stream below freshened the air, making the flames dance and the bed of ashes glow bright red and yellow. He turned and looked at Norpisia as she sat there quietly chewing her olpurda. When it crossed his mind that he and Norpisia were at that moment isolated in the middle of the wilderness, he feared for her safety. While such isolation was nothing new to him having lived a nomadic lifestyle most of his life, he knew Norpisia's parents lived a semi-sedentary life. He was therefore, worried about her ability to persevere the harsh experience that she was inevitably going to be exposed to until they reached Nkararo. Her capability to endure prolonged periods of solitude in the wilderness also worried him. He sorrowfully recalled how his departed sister struggled, with little success, to cope with loneliness as they went through the rough terrain. Now that Norpisia was married to him, he reasoned, she had to learn to cope with the kind of life he lived.

At first, he did not know how to explain to Norpisia that it was important for him to keep an all night vigil in the cattle enclosure to protect the animals from attacks by lions or hyenas; that they would neither find time to chat in the evenings nor have time to spend together until they got to Nkararo. While he kept vigil at the cattle enclosure, he expected her to be alert in the *olngoborr* that was adjacent to the calves, sheep and goats. He knew that leopards were a menace at night for they were fond of goat and sheep meat.

When he eventually gathered courage and broached the subject, explaining to her the need to undertake the measures he had in mind, Kedoki was utterly surprised that, Norpisia did not fret. So, when Kedoki left and went to his vigil, Norpisia curled-up under her blanket and thought longingly of her warm bed at her mother's house in Olomuruti. In the *olngoborr* the ground was hard and cold and her threadbare blanket and the *lesos* she wore felt thin and unable to protect her from the cold wind blowing against her back. The fire made a soft crackling sound, the ashes settled, the coal glowed dark red and then amber as the wind blew across it. She reached out of the blanket and threw more pieces of firewood onto the fire. She then pulled back her arm under the blanket and drew the edge of it up over her ears and settled back. She closed her eyes and began to contemplate the kind of life into which her marriage to Kedoki had catapulted her.

Ordinarily, she thought that marriage would have put her into a comfortable homestead, taking care of her house, milking the cows in the morning and in the evening, and making sure that her children and her husband were well fed. But in this wilderness in which she found herself, she would have to live a life of adventure. She knew she would have to face all kinds of danger. But luckily, she told herself, the training that she had had at her grandmother's home would be handy in coping with any eventuality in this wilderness. She promised herself that she would fully help Kedoki to rear and protect their cattle and ensure that she filled the slots left by the deaths of his brother and sister. She knew she had a dual role to play not only as a wife but also as a worthy companion. Not used to sleeping in the open, sleep eluded her the whole night.

She was up before daylight the following morning. She rubbed her eyes vigorously as she yawned widely, and stumbled on a pile of firewood that stood next to the *olngoborr*. She broke some twigs from the pile, and tossed them into the fire. After that, she knelt by the fire gently and blew onto it. Immediately, a cheerful bright flame flared and she placed a pot of milk over it. The milk had just boiled when Kedoki came in followed by hungry dogs that yawned, stretched and stood shivering in the frosty morning air.

"*Supa enkitok-ai nanyorr,*" he greeted her cheerfully as he sat on a flat stone next to the fire. "How was the night?"

"*Epa-oiye olpayian-lai,*" she answered demurely. "The night was very cold but peaceful."

"Did you hear any strange noises at night?" he asked her, fearing that she could have been scared by the hyenas that tried several times to enter into the cattle enclosure.

"No, I didn't," she answered as she handed him a mugful of steaming milk. "Only an occasional cow-bell tinkled."

"Hyenas attempted to get into the cattle enclosure several times at night," he told her concernedly. "I did not sleep a wink!"

"Do you ever sleep?" she asked sympathetically. "What a difficult task it is taking care of such a large herd alone!"
"It was better when my brother was still alive," he said as he flinched from the memory of his departed brother. "We used to alternate in keeping vigil."

"From tonight henceforth," she said emotionally but with a firm assertion in her voice, "I will take the place of your departed brother. Tonight I shall keep vigil and you will sleep."

"Never!" he answered, vehemently opposing her proposal, "You will not put your life at risk while I snore under a warm blanket inside the *olngoborr*."

As Kedoki spoke, Norpisia recalled an incident at her grandmother's home when hyenas entered into the sheep's pen and disembowelled ten of them. When her grandmother, who was away at that time, returned and was informed of the mishap, she was angry and railed at her derogatorily, telling her she was a useless weakling who could not defend sheep against predators.

Norpisia was so agitated by the accusation that she seriously took up the challenge, and for the next ten nights, she kept vigil outside her grandmother's sheep pen, spear and sword in her hands waiting patiently for hyenas to enter into the snare she had set. And for the ten nights that followed, she killed a hyena every night. It was only after avenging her grandmother's dead sheep that she felt vindicated.

"Just try me, and if you find me wanting, you can withdraw me from the vigil," she pleaded with him. "After all, I left all that I love in order to be with you and help you."

After much persuasion, Kedoki gave in. Norpisia let him rest as she went about with the morning chores.

Within no time, she had milked the cows, let out the calves, kids and lambs to suckle, and she had fed the dogs. After she had loaded the donkeys, she awoke him to prepare to drive the herd to the pastures. And with that, a routine was established that they followed in their long sojourn in the wilderness while on their way to Nkararo in Olorukoti.

They drove the herd southwards from the last night camping site. As usual, Kedoki walked ahead of the cattle, restraining them from moving fast so that they grazed without tiring themselves. Norpisia brought up the rear, ensuring that young kids, lambs and calves were not left behind.

As they herded their animals across the Ilaikipiak plains, their entire view, from one end of the plains to the other, was of a vast encompassing grassland. The rich tawny grass that was constantly in rippling motion, stretched as far as the eye could see. The few trees that dotted the expansive plain only helped to accentuate the dominant vegetation. Grazing contentedly across the plains were herds of thousands of zebras and wildebeests. There were also the close-packed, gracefully horned gazelles with their ever wagging tails. In addition, giraffes arched their long necks as they nibbled leaves on tree-tops. Norpisia noticed the cow-like elands with their dewlaps swaying and wondered what kind of calves would be born if their cows were crossed with bulls from their cattle. Grazing beside the elands were thousands of the red, lyre-horned impala with their little tails twitching incessantly. Not far from the herbivorous animals were the carnivorous ones that were always stalking them. There were the hunting cheetahs, the ungainly hyenas and the silver-backed jackals that kept a watchful vigil, always hoping to catch any of the herbivorous unawares. And not far away were lions, the kings of the wilderness.

Norpisia had just stopped to pick up an exhausted

lamb that was unable to walk, when she faced her first real scare in the wilderness. She was hurrying to catch up with the herd after walking back to collect the extremely tired lamb when she saw a procession of four rhinos: a large male, a female and two half-grown calves, walking in a single file, the heads of the grown-up animals weighed down by their curved horns. When the big male scented Norpisia, he halted and swung a lowered head around to face her, pawing the ground furiously with one big foot while preparing to charge. Norpisia's stared helplessly at the aggressive beast, her feet rooted on the ground. She, however, did not lose her senses, for when the frightening monster finally charged, hurtling towards her with lightning speed, Norpisia took off like a shot, running for dear life. She screamed as she ran toward the cattle. Once she disappeared among the herd, the rhino screeched to a halt having lost Norpisia's scent. It pawed the ground angrily, turned and ran back to join the rest of the rhinos before disappearing down the valley.

On hearing Norpisia's scream, Kedoki swung into action, running with his spear raised high and ready. He found her crouching under a thicket.

"A rhino nearly killed me," she said nervously as she trembled, tears streaming down her contorted face.

"It is all right now, I'm here," he assured her soothingly. "The cowardly beast should have faced me instead of running away."

She explained what happened, while he listened attentively. When she looked up and saw the concern in his gleaming eyes, she felt reassured. An aura of invincibility enveloped her and she confidently felt safe around him. She felt relieved knowing that he cared for her and that he would always protect and provide for her. While standing with him there under the tree, she realized for the first time that deep in her heart, she loved him more than she could express herself.

The incident shocked Kedoki. When he first heard her scream, he responded the same way he always did when there was an emergency – a leopard attacking a sheep or a goat and he having to run and forcefully retrieve it from the beast. But when he found her crying and trembling under a thicket, yearning for his re-assurance, he at once realized how much she meant to him. It dawned on him that he had to secure her safety and her well-being. It also dawned on him that he loved her more than he ever believed possible. Until then, he did not know he could love so much, let alone think that he nearly lost her to the beast.

From then henceforth, he declared, his eye would always be on her and for the first time since they became husband and wife, they held hands affectionately as they walked together back to where their livestock grazed peacefully.

CHAPTER 4

Norpisia was getting used to the arduous life in the wilderness. The period out there was so eventful that it was difficult to imagine that it had taken them a month to cross the expansive Laikipiak plains. The open grassland of gently rolling hills through which they were now traversing as they grazed their flock was gaining elevation. Kedoki told her they were now approaching the Enkare-Narok river.

As the banks of the river rose in eminence, the vegetation changed too, and to Norpisia's relief, the grass became shorter. She was happier and felt safer because she preferred being able to see her surroundings clearly. In the plain, where the grass was so tall that she could hardly see the sheep and goats as they grazed, hyenas were a menace. They killed and dragged away a number of sheep without her noticing. That had upset her so much.

"Don't get so upset, my lovely wife," Kedoki told her soothingly when he found her crying after a hyena had killed and dragged away one of the sheep. "The war with the hyenas is not over yet!"

"To think that they can just walk in and devour our sheep!" she cried in agitation.

"Calm down, my love," he told her calmly. "We shall soon be out of the plains and to an area where we can see them as they approach." Kedoki knew as much as Norpisia did, the attachment they had to their cattle. Despite the number of animals they owned, they knew each one of them individually. They loved each one of them as they would love a child. They had reared them, treating them when they were sick and protecting them from predators and rustlers. They had shared the isolation in the wilderness and had grown close as any creatures that were dissimilar could ever be. The cattle knew, understood and trusted them. Humans and animals lived a symbiotic life.

On seeing Norpisia weeping for the loss of a sheep that was killed by the hyenas, Kedoki understood her anxiety. He shared her feelings of devastation and loss.

"One day we shall get to Nkararo," Kedoki told Norpisia as they watched the animals graze contentedly. "Then I'll settle you in a secure homestead and you will live in a house built with your own hands."

Norpisia listened keenly to him, and Kedoki watched a gentle smile soften her face.

"You speak as gently as my grandmother used to," she told him pleasantly. "In fact, had she known I was going to get married to a man like you, she would have been delighted. Certainly, she would have liked you."

She looked at him adoringly. The short period she had lived with him in the wilderness had given her ample time to observe him more closely. She appreciatively thought Enkai had been generous to him with his gifts; a rare intelligence that gave him the understanding of the physical aspects of the terrain they were traversing, skills in making weapons such as bows and arrows, knobkerries and others, and he had mastered the art of improvisation. He made useful things out of unlikely items.

The two drove their herd slowly toward the slope in the direction of the river. The cattle seemed to enjoy the short thick grass that grew in selected areas of ample moisture. They grazed ardently along the river they had been following. They came upon a broad valley with a gentle grassy slope, leading to a swift river that was flowing down a waterfall. At the base of the waterfall were strewn stones of various types and sizes, ranging from large boulders to fine sandy gravel. The rocky course was bare of vegetation, scoured by the incessant rapid water flow. They found the area near the river much cooler. As the afternoon wore into the evening, they began to look for a suitable place to set up camp. They had just settled on a place when Kedoki pointed Norpisia to something across the river. Before she could get to see what he was pointing at, a loud, blast rent the air. She dashed to his side.

A large herd of elephants were milling about with great agitation near the edge of the tall grass at the riverside. Apparently, they had sensed human scent and were trying to spot them.

The awesome mammals were of all ages and sizes. Kedoki later explained from a safer place that the herd comprised related females that included mothers, daughters, sisters and their off-springs. He pointed out an old huge matriarch who, he said, led the herd.

Norpisia noted that the overall colour of the elephants appeared to be reddish brown but on closer look, she observed many variations of the basic shade. The big animals had long curved tusks. After sometime, they either lost the scent, or they lost interest, for they turned their attention back to tearing out trunkfuls of tall grass in a steady rhythm.

Kedoki and Norpisia left their hide-out, went to re-group the cattle and drove them to the spot where they were to camp for the night. As she got closer to the cattle, Norpisia noticed the white birds that were constant companions of the cattle. They adroitly avoided to be trampled upon, while feeding on the insects that fled the path of the animals and ticks as they grazed.

She was looking at the birds when she suddenly felt a strange sensation pass through her body. She quickly looked across the river where the elephants were and noticed that they had stopped grazing. Some of them raised their heads facing the direction from which a strange sound emanated, their large ears flapping furiously. Suddenly, the old matriarch roared; a deep vibrating rumble. Norpisia, first felt a chill, then the rise of goose-pimples on her body as a low growl that sounded like the rumbling of thunder, came from the forest where the elephants were.

"Norpisia-ai," Kedoki called urgently, "Look beyond the elephants across the river and see who is coming!"

Norpisia looked across the river, and hurtling down toward the herd of elephants, was a huge male elephant with fantastic and immense, upward curving tusks. When he reached the clearing, the other elephants ran toward him, squealing, trumpeting and rumbling their greetings. They surrounded him, trying to touch him with their trunks. Norpisia was awed as she watched the giant bull. He held his head high, and proudly displayed his pair of ivory. Towering nearly two feet above the matriarch, and nearly twice the weight of the other females, he was by far the most gigantic elephant Norpisia had ever seen.

"*Eitu aikata adol oltome obanji,*" Norpisia exclaimed, remarking that she had never before seen an elephant of that size.

"*Enkingasia ogirae!*" Kedoki shouted back saying the animal was awesome.

That evening, as she boiled mutton for their evening meal, Norpisia still thought of the elephants. Although she had seen many elephants at Olomuruti before, she had not observed them that closely.

That afternoon, she had been amazed at the dexterity and strength of the elephants' trunks. She had watched as each one of them wrapped the muscular trunk around a bunch of tall grass, then held it together while the upper digit fingered more stems that were growing nearby into its clutch, until it had accumulated a sizeable amount.

The trunk then yanked the grass out of the ground, roots and all. It shook off the soil from the roots then stuffed it all into its mouth, and while chewing, reached for some more. She noticed that they had created a large clearing of the tall grass and concluded that a herd could quickly strip a considerable area of vegetation.

When Kedoki came to the *olngoborr* for his piece of boiled mutton that evening, Norpisia initiated a conversation about the elephants. She wondered whether the elephants' feeding habits were not a threat to the environment, seeing the damage that a herd had left behind as it made its migration across the savannah lands.

"The elephants may appear ruinous to the environment," Kedoki answered "but what I've observed over the years is that for all the grass ripped and barks stripped from trees, there is a benefit. By clearing the old, tall grass and small stunted trees, fresh seed are sown and grow to feed our cattle and other animals."

"Who sows?" asked Norpisia, surprised.

"You can't imagine who Enkai has given the burden of sowing the seeds," Kedoki answered mirthfully. "Do you know the little *olmoilaa* called *olobel-kik?*"

"The dung-beetle?" Norpisia asked, her interest in the subject growing intensely. "I don't see how the ignoble *olobel-kik*, that ignominiously burrows and wallows in the dung could have the honourable duty of sowing the seeds."

"You see, elephants spend most of the day and night

36

eating," Kedoki explained. "They eat shreds of bark torn off trees with their tusks. They gather tree branches with their seeds and devour them. The roughage consumed every day is extracted through dung within a day. And with it, the grass seeds, tree seeds and other plants are dropped undigested."

"And then?" asked Norpisia, entranced.

"This is where *olobel-kik*, the dung-beetle comes in," Kedoki said laughing uproariously. "Our little friend turns the dung upside down, digs up the soil underneath and buries seeds that germinate merrily when it rains."

"Wonderful!" exclaimed Norpisia. She wrinkled her nose as she imagined the strong, pungent smell of the dung that the dung-beetle wallowed in, in order to plant the seeds. "I see. From now henceforth, I shall endeavour to respect the beetle," she said to conclude the discussion.

Later at night as he kept vigil beside the fire in the cattle enclosure, Kedoki thought of the various types of herbivorous that competed for grass with the cattle in the savannah. Besides elephants and rhinos, there were elands, zebras, wildebeests and the smaller antelopes. Of all, Kedoki assessed, it was the wildebeest that rivalled the cattle. Although they were all herbivorous, he knew some grazers did not eat precisely the same type of grass. They had different digestive systems, different feeding habits and had developed subtly different adaptations. While rhinos and elephants were sustained by highly fibrous stems and barks from trees, wildebeests, like cattle, needed grass to survive. He knew the wildebeests, like nomads, migrated from one area to another in pursuit of the nutritious short savannah grass.

He recalled once seeing them crossing the flooded Mara river in thousands, as they ventured into the southern grasslands in search of the green, fresh grass that sprouted after the rains. What a spectacular scene! He recalled with a reminiscent smile, how he stood there entranced at the breathtaking view before his eyes. The scene was still so fresh in his mind that he could still see the wildebeests with their compact sturdy bodies as they jumped into the water, as if pushed into it by a power they could not resist. They struggled against a strong tide, their heavily built chests and shoulders rippling, as they swum across the swiftly flowing river. They jostled in the water, pushing one another with their large heads that were protected by their massive short black horns. Some of them were killed by crocodiles that waited for them at the edge of the water. Those that managed to cross the river crowded together at the riverbank, as they struggled to run uphill. As they scrambled, their small hooves raised red dust that covered them, making them look as if they were engulfed in a ball of fire.

By the time the wildebeests returned from the southern grassland, they had multiplied. And the young calves had flourished, not only because of the abundance of rich green grass in that region, but also because of the variety of grass species available in the rain drenched grassland.

It was only around a small village called Oloisuya, remembered Kedoki, where the inhabitants had cut down trees indiscriminately and burnt charcoal, that the grass cover was thin and short. The wind had eroded deeper gullies on the dry land, and in the upper valley of a perennial river, the riverbed had gone dry, sending the people there packing, to look for water elsewhere.

While Kedoki sat in the cold night contemplating life in the expansive savannah land, Norpisia lay inside the olngoborr thinking about her past. It was completely dark under those hides that made up the outer covering of the oblong temporary shelter. Not the faintest hint of a silhouette or dark shadow could be discerned against the surrounding background, except for a faint redness from the lingering coals in the fireplace.

Unable to sleep inside the *olngoborr*, Norpisia got up and took her blanket with her, and proceeded to make her bed next to the fire outside the temporary shelter. She lay awake under the starlit sky, staring at the patterns of the constellations while listening to the usual sounds of the night. She could hear the wind blowing and sifting through the trees; the gurgle of the river as it ran down over the boulders; the chirrup of crickets and cicadas; the irritating croak of frogs; and the eerie hoots of an owl. From a distant, she heard the deep frightening roar of a lion and a loud trumpet of an elephant.

Her mind flew back to Olomuruti where she was born and brought up. Happy and sad memories were all tied up there in a bundle. She realized that the sad

39

memories surfaced in her mind faster than the good ones did. She was still grieving the loss: her siblings, her playmates, and the villagers who were all killed by the bandits. Oblivious to the tears flowing down her cheeks, she heaved great sobs to release her sorrows.

She thought of the man who had become her husband. He was grieving too, having lost his brother and sister. He was, however, strong and had accepted his loss stoically. She wished she could emulate him.

Her brief nap was interrupted by a sudden noise. Alert and tense, she lay still, trying to find out what woke her. She first heard the barking of a dog then a loud snuffling behind the olngoborr. She knew there was an intruder in the enclosure. Stealthily she got up, picked a spear and stood waiting in readiness. Then she heard some movement, snuffling sounds from somewhere between the fireplace and the tree over which she had placed the remainder of the mutton. Then the barking of the dogs intensified as they bravely faced the intruder. From the cattle enclosure, the donkeys brayed nervously.

Kedoki heard the commotion and ran fast towards the *olngoborr*, his spear raised. Amid vicious snarls, a rumbling growl and a yelp of pain from a bitten dog, bright sparks flew around a large shape that stumbled into the fireplace. Kedoki guessed that the intruder could be a hyena possibly attracted by the mutton that Norpisia had hung on a tree near the *olngoborr*. Then, he heard a swishing sound of as object swiftly cut through the air. An instant thud was immediately followed by a howl, and a deafening crashing noise as the beast ran through the trees.

"I am certain my spear has hit the hyena," Norpisia said confidently, "I hope I have hit it at the right place."

"What a markswoman you are my love!" Kedoki exclaimed in astonishment. "You are also a courageous and worthy companion."

Norpisia smiled at him pleasantly. She had sworn that she was going to take the place of his slain brother and help him protect their cattle.

He then walked to the fireplace to examine the trail.

"I think the beast is losing a lot of blood," he said as he stooped low to look at the trail of blood on the grass. "I don't think it will survive."

"We shall track it down in the morning," Norpisia said enthusiastically. "If I've killed it, I'll be happy to have avenged the sheep its kith and kin killed in the plains."

"Norpisia, you are a courageous woman!" he told her excitedly. "But be careful the way you approach dangerous animals. I was worried about you. That animal could have hurt you."

Kedoki heard her sudden shudder and he glanced at her. She turned to look at him and their eyes, equally zealous in seeking to please one another locked for a moment. They both understood that with such a long journey ahead of them in the wilderness, it would be risky for Norpisia to get pregnant. They, therefore, avoided being physically close. Nevertheless, their feelings toward one another were becoming stronger and intimate.

As they stood side by side, Kedoki felt a quickening in his loins as he stared at Norpisia. On her part, Norpisia felt a pleasant sensation in her heart. The excitement she felt dissipated her strength and made her limbs weak. Her languorous half-open eyes looked up at him suggestively, her mouth slightly open as she took quick short breaths. Kedoki looked at her for a moment as though he did not understand her body language. He felt overwhelmed by his love for her, but his disciplined background restrained him. He relaxed, gave her a hug and then stepped back, smiling ruefully.

"Our first duty is to our herd," he told her sheepishly. "We shall have all the time to ourselves when we finally get home at Nkararo."

When Kedoki found the dead hyena in the bush the following morning, with her spear having penetrated its rib-cage and pierced its heart, he was full of praises for Norpisia.

"That's what I love about you, Norpisia," he told her guardedly. "You are always full of surprises that go beyond my wildest imagination. Who would have ever thought that a woman could throw a spear so forcefully as you did?"

She radiated with satisfaction of his praises and approval of what she had done. However, she knew that there were many more things, beside killing hyenas, that she knew, having learnt them from her grandmother, and which she could show him but was afraid of doing, lest he got alarmed. She had seen his first reaction when he saw the way her spear penetrated into the hyenas rib-cage. He had looked at her strangely. Fear welled up in her, thinking that he may consider her a witch, a woman with supernatural powers who could easily kill him and take away his fortune.

Kedoki's thoughts were, nonetheless, completely different. The deep and intimate relationship that was evolving with Norpisia, opened new vistas in his life, which he had never thought existed. His attitude towards women had been, until he met Norpisia, dismissive, regarding them as a gender of little consequence, required only for the purpose of procreation. He had therefore, surprisingly found the relationship with her to be a totally different experience.

They were about to cross Enkare-Narok river. Kedoki stood watching his herd of cattle graze contentedly. Now that they were about to leave the grasslands and enter the bushy stretch, before they ventured into the dense forest, he was worried about the dangers that he knew lurked in that region. Despite the expected challenges, he felt ready to venture into the next phase of the journey through the wilderness.

CHAPTER 5

Six months after crossing the Enkare-Narok river, Norpisia, Kedoki and their herd were still in its vicinity. The magnificent grasslands of that flat southern region pleased Kedoki. A rich new growth, unusual at that time of the year, burgeoned across the open landscape. A heavy downpour of flooding rains, exceptional in its timing, was responsible for the bluish green rich grass called *olperesi* that rippled in the breeze like waves on the wide river, and which the cattle loved to graze. The rains brought a resurgent to the woodlands of not only the grass, but many other colourful blooms such as *osenetoi* with its deep yellow multipetalled tiny flowers and the spotted pink lilies called *esukutari* whose flowers were tinted in various colours from yellow and orange to red and purple.

They stayed close to the river as they journeyed on. Kedoki was almost certain that the course of the river was making a turn to the west, but he worried that it might only be a wide swing in its general meandering. He had already decided that if the course of the river changed, they would stop following it and find their own way across the woodlands first and thereafter, through the dense forest in the highlands.

On that particular day, he had spotted several places that could have been suitable for their nightly stop-over. But Kedoki was looking for a particular site, where he had been told other sojourners regularly stopped for the night as they crossed the woodland. It was the landmark he needed to verify their location and confirm that they had not lost direction. When they finally located the place that was situated on a hill, as usual, Kedoki built a kraal of thorn branches while Norpisia erected her olngoborr and set everything ready for the night.

The sun was setting and the sunbeams on the western horizon were golden red, tinged with purple, giving the surrounding clouds a bluish red hue. The stands of deep forest and open pastures blended together in the distant. The breeze from the river was very refreshing. However, when the wind blew from the direction of the cattle enclosure, it brought an acrid smell of dust from the trampled area around the sheep fold and from the kraal.

When Kedoki walked into the *olngoborr's* area carrying a load of firewood, he noted that Norpisia was not her usual self. Something seemed to worry her. He dropped the load of firewood, then looked at the dogs that were lying beside the fireplace. He snapped his fingers and signalled them to follow him. They quickly leapt up and trotted behind him as he led them back to the cattle enclosure where he kept his usual nightly vigil.

As he sat there silently, he thought of Norpisia, and wondered what could be worrying her. After concluding that he could not possibly be the cause of her apparent temperament, he accepted that as a woman, Norpisia was entitled to an occasional outburst of anger and a moody stubbornness. To try to appease and brighten her mood, he walked out into the bushes in the waning light and looked for ripe *ilamuriak* juicy fruits, which he knew she loved and wrapped them in broad leaves.

When darkness fell, Norpisia tossed more firewood into the fire. After it flared, the dogs became visible on the edge of the firelight as they walked back from the cattle enclosure, and waited hungrily to be fed. Norpisia took some meat from a carcass and threw chunks to each one of them. They snapped up greedily.

By the time Kedoki returned for his evening meal, he found an appetizing chunk of mutton spitting over the flames, the outer layer of fat sizzling. He planted his spear on the ground and sat on a log. Norpisia observed that there was something that he held with his other hand that he kept behind his back.

"Whatever you are roasting smells good," he said trying to cheer her up. "Is it about to be ready? I'm starving."

"It's actually ready," she said nonchalantly. Then she suddenly asked with a measure of curiosity, "What are you hiding behind your back?"

"Nothing really," he said trying to charm her. "Well, it just happened that when I was rounding up the cattle, I found something sweet in the bushes. If you promise to be good, I might give you some!"

"Give me what?" she asked with little interest.

He brought forth his cupped hand and unwrapped the broad leaves to reveal the golden colour ripe fruits.

"Big, juicy, sweet *ilamuriak* fruits," he said smilingly as he proffered the fruit to her.

Norpisia's eyes lit up. "Oh, I love *ilamuriak*!"

"Don't you think I know it?" he asked with a twinkle in his eye. "But what do I get in return for my effort?"

She took the fruits from his hand and did not excitedly pop them into her mouth as he expected her to do. Instead, she held them in her hand and stared at him with a strange vacant look in her eyes.

"What is it?" He asked with urgency. "Is anything the matter?"

"Nothing," she answered demurely, her eyes downcast. "Nothing to worry you."

"Surely, if something is worrying you," he said heatedly, "don't you think I should know about it?"

She gave in and finally told him. She had been haunted by a horrible dream the previous night. It had set her wondering whether the power of clairvoyance which she had not experienced ever since she got married to Kedoki, was re-asserting itself in her. It all started the previous night when sleep eluded her. She tossed and turned most of the night. When she eventually dozed off, she had a fitful sleep that was interrupted several times by a scaring horrible dream.

She dreamt that a lion had jumped over the thorn fence of their cattle enclosure and got into the midst of the cattle. It roared thunderously as it went for the jugular

47

vein of a heifer, sending the rest of the cattle into panic that caused a stampede. They tore out of the enclosure and scattered into the dark night in all directions. The sheep also stirred in confusion, bleating and bobbing their heads as they ran around in circles.

Then, she saw Kedoki emerge from a bush holding his spear aloft ready to face the beast. The lion bared its fangs in a horrible fierce snarl, its eyes shining like green emeralds. It growled as it leapt to tear him into shreds. He gallantly walked toward the advancing lion, his valour doing little to daunt the beast. As the two faced off, the dream grew hazy. Kedoki was fading away and she panicked. She called out his name and pleaded with him not to leave her alone in the wilderness. But he did not listen to her. In an instant he was gone. She called out again but he had faded away into the horizon.

Feeling desolate, she cried desperately. She wished he had left her with something of his own to cling onto and for which to remember him. It was as if she was floating on water and desperately needed something to hold onto. She felt an overwhelming sorrow in her heart. Suddenly, she heard the voice of her grandmother urgently urging her to run fast and get out of the woodland and head to the forest in the highlands. She told her to go up the hills and team up with elephants, rhinos, lions and other animals, and courageously face a greedy multi-headed monster that was on its way to the forest, to destroy and devour it, leaving the whole land dry and bare.

The roar of a real lion in the nearby forest awoke

her, and she had found herself trembling and sweating profusely.

"Oh, my dear husband," cried Norpisia as she clung onto him, still feeling the desolation. "It was terrible. It was frightening seeing you facing the huge deadly lion."

"It is all right," he reassured her.

His reassurance calmed her nerves a little. But Kedoki hardly knew what Norpisia had learnt about dreams from her grandmother. Before she had moved to her grandmother's home, she had known what all other children of her village knew about dreams. They were either good or bad dreams. Bad dreams were sanitized and were given positive meanings. If one dreamt of dead or dying relatives, they were said to be having a fabulous time. On the other hand, if one dreamt of a good time, especially at a feast where meat was being eaten in large quantities, then as sure as day followed night, death and destruction were said to follow. There was, however, a safety valve: if one told of a bad dream to someone the following day after it happened, it lessened the possibilities of it coming to pass.

It was different with her grandmother. She was an *enkoiboni*, and dreams were her stock-in-trade. During the time Norpisia lived with her, she encouraged her to remember each of her dreams in detail and preserve them in her mind. Norpisia often sat with her grandmother as she analyzed her dreams. She had special pebbles that she used to discern the meanings of dreams. To her consternation, her grandmother's divinations after

49

analyzing her dreams, were often correct. Events foreseen came to pass without fail. Sometimes, she lit a smoky fire and amidst the smoky mist that made tears run down their faces, she went into lengthy loud incantations, calling upon spirits to reveal the meanings of their dreams.

Her dream the previous night, where her husband faded fast into the horizon, made her feel anxious and worried. What did it portend? What about that part of her dream where her heart ached with sorrows, wishing she had something of his to hold on, something for which to remember him for, something to touch? What did that mean? Did it have anything to do with her not having his child in the event anything happened to him? How she wished her grandmother was there to discern the meaning of the dream. But could her grandmother reverse the beckon of fate? She recalled her grandmother telling an old man: An arrow does not miss a man destined to die.

She remembered one particular incident when an old man arrived at her grandmother's home very early in the morning. He was panting breathlessly and his eyes were red and tearful. He sobbed and revealed his fearful dream again and again as her grandmother listened keenly. His dream was about his only son and heir, who in the dream was abducted by bandits and taken away together with all his livestock. His plea to her grandmother was to ensure the dream did not come to pass. The man was ready to pay any price to ensure he got the results that he desired.

Her grandmother lit her smoky fire after which she went into her incantations. At the end, she sorrowfully and tearfully told the old man that the die was cast and that the premonition was irreversible. It would come to pass. She, therefore, refused to take his money. And true to her divination, when the bandits struck a year later, the old man's son was abducted, never to be seen again. Would her dream about Kedoki come to pass? She wondered.

Long after Kedoki resumed duty at the cattle enclosure, Norpisia sat thoughtfully near the fire, its embers blinking flickeringly. She was still brooding about the dream when sleep overtook her.

The following morning, Norpisia woke up before the crack of dawn. She loved the cold mornings. From the melodies of bird-songs that had awakened her, she could distinguish the sharp elaborate call notes of *entinyoit* bird. Then, she heard a melodious warble that got louder and louder. When she could not locate the source of the thrilling song, Norpisia rolled on her side and saw the brown inconspicuous little *enkasero* just landing. The bird walked on the ground easily and quickly, well balanced by its large hind claws, then bobbed its small crested head in the nearby plants and came up with a caterpillar in its beak. With quick, jerky steps, it rushed toward a bare scrape in the ground near the stems of an *olobaai* bush, where a camouflaged cluster of newly hatched chicks, suddenly sprang to life, each opening its mouth begging to be filled with the delectable morsel.

Norpisia softly whistled, replicating the birdsong so precisely that the mother bird stopped feeding its chicks and momentarily turned in her direction, looking for another bird. Norpisia whistled again and the bird took a few steps toward her. When she lived with her grandmother, she taught her to imitate bird calls. When she had gained skill, she would call them and they would come expecting to see other birds of their kind.

Leaving the birds to themselves, Norpisia got up to attend to her morning chores. She lit the fire and heated their morning milk. She poured some into her mug, cupped her hands firmly round the mug to absorb the heat and sat warming herself by the fire as she drank her milk leisurely. She watched the sun wake up the Oloonderri ranges to the east of the valley. It began with the first pink hint of the pre-dawn light defining the top edge of the ridges, spreading slowly at first, reflecting a rosy glow in the east. Then suddenly, even before the edge of the glowing ball of fire sent a tentative gleam above the horizon, the blazing golden brown clouds nuzzled up against it, the way a pet would nuzzle its owner, heralding its heroic coming. Then it spread its glow everywhere, warming up the valley, which till then, was freezing cold.

As she sat in the comfort of the warm fire, and feeling her emotions flicker across her mind, Norpisia was engrossed into a contemplative mood. She knew how passionately she loved Kedoki and wanted to be with

52

him, preparing his meals, helping him tend and protect their herd. But she was getting worn out and sick of the wilderness. She longed to see her family. She was longing for human company. She wanted to meet people she would talk to, and laugh with. She did not want to think of Kedoki's people or how long they still had to travel before they reached his home. She even did not want to think about how they were going to cross the dense forest that Kedoki told her was teeming with dangerous animals. All she wanted was to be with other human beings beside Kedoki.

In the past few days, she had caught herself looking up at the distant hills, hoping to see sojourners who would probably be traveling to Olomuruti. Anyone who would break the monotony would be welcome.

That afternoon, to her utter astonishment and surprise, she saw two men, at a distance sauntering toward her. She had left Kedoki standing under a giant tree watching the cattle graze, while she went to the nearby river to fetch water. He turned when he heard her whistling in the manner she did whenever she detected a dangerous animal. He turned and saw her running up the hill toward him, the sheet she wore flying behind her like wings of a bird. Her expression was tense and excited as she waved her hand in the air beckoning him to meet her half way. He armed himself with his spear and knobkerrie and hurried toward her.

"What is it?" Kedoki asked in panic.

"I have seen two men walking toward us," she answered unable to hide the excitement in her emotion-filled voice. "I have seen them with my two eyes."

Kedoki walked down the slope briskly with his spear held firmly in his hand, while Norpisia, a bow and two arrows in her hand, and a quiver dangling down her shoulder, followed behind him. He scanned the area while sheltering his eyes with his hand against the glare of the sun. But there was no one in sight. Norpisia pointed toward the forest line below the crest on the other side of the hill. Kedoki nodded and glanced back at the cattle that were still grazing contentedly. Then, he stood and motioned Norpisia to his side. They both waited anxiously, watching the line of foliage. A moment later two men came out of the bushes and walked toward them. Suddenly, the dogs came running, fiercely barking at the advancing men. Kedoki whistled, calming the dogs down, as he stared at the approaching men searchingly. He noted that one of the men was of his age or older while the other was a tall youth, possibly one who had just been shaven after initiation.

"*Ara Masintet!*" Kedoki suddenly called loudly after recognizing the older man and strode toward him. "It is Kedoki."

"*Kedoki lenkaji e yeiyo!*" the man exclaimed dumbfounded. "We never expected to meet you in this wilderness."

They hugged each other excitedly. Then, the man Kedoki called Masintet backed off and looked at Kedoki intently, holding him by the shoulders. "I can't believe it's you and not your ghost."

All that time, Norpisia watched the expression on the young man's face as the older men greeted one another boisterously. His expression changed from that of puzzlement to that of distant recognition. Kedoki hugged Masintet one more time as the two laughed. Norpisia noted the genuine affection they shared.

Kedoki turned his attention to the young man who Masintet introduced as his younger brother; Lembarta. Kedoki proffered his hand and the two barely touched each other's palms. Lembarta seemed a little embarrassed, as he greeted Kedoki silently. On his part, Kedoki understood the reluctance. Lembarta must have been a boy six years earlier when he left their village at Eorr-Narasha to take their cattle in pursuit of pastures. He was, therefore, a stranger to the young man and exuberant displays of unrestrained affections, that he showed Masintet, were out of question in his case. He introduced the two men to his wife Norpisia, and the young man knitted his brows in consternation as he looked at Norpisia, a woman armed with bows and arrows, like a man. Masintet chuckled heartily as he looked at Norpisia and then Kedoki. Kedoki cleared his throat, feeling suddenly defensive. But not wanting to discuss her in her presence, he told Norpisia to go with Lembarta and select a sheep for slaughter while he talked to Masintet.

"I hope you have not become another Lesiote?"

Masintet told Kedoki as he slapped him on his shoulder cheerfully while roaring with hearty laughter. "Who is this lass then, who looks half man, half woman?"

"How can I be another Lesiote?" asked Kedoki with an incredulous look on his face.

The two men knew well the story of the legendary Lesiote. The poor man was the butt of bawdy jokes told by one generation after the other. He was said to have driven their cattle with his father to far away lands in pursuit of pastures, and remained in the wilderness from the time he was a small boy, until he became an adult. He underwent all the rites of passage while in the wilderness. It was said he had not had a chance to meet a woman until his father brought him one to marry. He received the girl cordially and the two developed a friendship. They went out looking after cattle and together they fought threatening wild animals. However, not once did Lesiote get intimate with the girl. The girl wondered what kind of man Lesiote was.

One day, she decided to find out what the man felt about her. In the evening after drinking their milk, the girl took off her *olokesena*, the wrap-around skirt that women wore, and walked to him naked. Lesiote was shocked and could not believe his eyes. He stared at her with incredulity, his eyes dilated, his mouth agape with his lips hanging loose. Suddenly and without warning, he let out a loud yell as he bolted out of the hut at lightning speed and headed for his father's hut.

"Father, Father," he called urgently as he panted

56

breathlessly. "The man you brought me to be my companion is suffering from a terrible disease that has eaten away his manhood!"

"You God forsaken fool!" his father was said to have thundered angrily. "Have you no imagination? It is no wonder your mother named you lesiote!"

Kedoki cleared his throat again and looked up at Masintet's twinkling smile. He shrugged his shoulders self-consciously as he said, "I want to assure you the woman you saw is certainly not half-man, half-woman. She is a real woman and she is my wife."

Masintet looked up at Kedoki, nodded and then chuckled in response to his explanation. "It is odd seeing a woman carrying a bow and arrows, with a quiver dangling down her shoulders, like a man. Kind of weird, isn't she?"

"You can hardly fault this woman," Kedoki explained seriously. "She is certainly a product of our environment, and she is only responding to the harsh life in this wilderness." He explained to his friend the circumstances that led him to seek the hand of Norpisia, not only as a wife but also as his worthy companion. He had lost his brother and his sister after they were attacked by bandits who stole part of his livestock. The same bandits, he told him, also killed a brother and a sister to the Norpisia. The two, therefore, shared common grief and bitterness. And they were only a small part of many families in that area who suffered brutality and cruelty in the hands of the heartless bandits. The brutes did not spare the life of anyone who came their way. They indiscriminately killed children, women and men, and herded off their livestock. In a nutshell, life in the north where he had been was ruthless, bestial and short.

"I swear, if I had power," Kedoki growled angrily, "I would gather and mobilize all able-bodied men to defend the defenceless people against the bandits!"

Kedoki turned and saw Norpisia approaching, in the company of Lembarta, bringing along a ram for slaughter and his hard look softened.

"If you say my woman is half-man just because she is courageous and dependable," he said smilingly, "then, I would agree with you entirely. During the period I have been with her, she had requited my trust in her appropriately by facing all manner of danger fearlessly."

"But don't you think you have behaved like Lesiote?" Masintet asked humorously. "Otherwise, how do you explain the fact that the two of you have been living together all this time and she is not with child?"

"On that front, I am like Lesiote," Kedoki said amidst uproarious laughter, "Only in my case, it is by design and not through ignorance!"

"In that case, I have come at the right time to rescue you from your self-imposed abstinence," he chuckled mischievously. "I am here to create an atmosphere of peace that will allow the two of you to bring forth a progeny that will in future join its generation to conceive viable ideas that will help wipe out the malady that breeds insecurity!"

"The founder said: 'God does not eat what man eats'," Kedoki enthused. "And that is the reason why it will not take long before God raises a man or woman who will one day stop the killing of innocent children, women and men; stop the destruction of their properties and bring about healing and lasting peace."

CHAPTER 6

Life in the wilderness took a dramatic turn with the arrival of the two brothers. It was only after their arrival that Kedoki realized how much isolation in the wilderness had weighed down Norpisia. After the death of his siblings, Kedoki had gone for weeks without seeing another person on the expansive pasturelands to the north of Olomuruti, and it didn't bother him. He had also become accustomed to the periodic stillness and silence in the bush. And as long as he had his herd safe, he did not care for anybody's company. The situation with Norpisia was however different. To worsen her desolation from the death of her siblings, their continued isolation in the wilderness had made her lonely and despondent. That was telling on her increasingly foul moods.

With the arrival of Masintet and Lembarta, she became animated as she excitedly narrated to them the unending woes that she had witnessed in the savannah lands. She found youthful company in Lembarta who was possibly her age. They had a lot in common, and they laughed away the hardships of the wilderness together. Lembarta had a friendly ingratiating manner and was perfect as a herdsman. He and his brother Masintet had heard from sojourners that Kedoki had lost his brother and sister to the bandits. They had also learnt that he had become very wealthy and that his herd and flock were so large that he was not able to drive them without assistance. Driven by the desire to own an additional cow, although they had their own back at home, the two brothers decided to grab the opportunity and ventured out hoping that they would find Kedoki in the wilderness. As they had expected, they found him in dire need of herdsmen. That being the case, they knew their assistance would earn them an *olekoisiayo*, at the end of the journey, which was the just wages that they expected for their labour.

While Lembarta spent his time with Norpisia, Kedoki enjoyed the endless stories that were humorously told by Masintet, the extrovert. Most of the time he shared his meals with him and he listened to him chattering as they ate. The three of them spent their nights at an *orripie*, a temporary wall built of tree branches, in the cattle enclosure, that shielded them from the severe cold wind that blew from the hills.

Everyday, they took the herd to graze. In the evenings, they first went to the olngoborr where Norpisia prepared their meals which they ate with a hearty gusto, thereafter, they retired to the cattle enclosure where to Kedoki's relief, they took turns in keeping vigil.

On one of the evenings, after he had eaten to his fill, Masintet sighed with complacency and tossing a couple of sticks into the fire looked at Kedoki thoughtfully. He said something that made Norpisia sit up.

"Wonders of the world will never cease, my friend," he said in his usual humorous tone. "Can you imagine animals ganging up to fight human beings?"

"What do you mean?" Kedoki asked, his eyebrows raised in puzzlement. "Animals conspired to fight humans? It's unheard of."

"It's happening right now," Masintet confirmed confidently. "Elephants, rhinos, buffaloes and hippopotamuses are trampling, goring and crushing people to death more often than before. They seem to be very angry with us, especially in areas where people have destroyed their habitat or where we have impeded their movement."

"But why have humans brought this calamity to themselves?" asked Kedoki, with a puzzled expression on his face. "Although humans and animals have from time immemorial been wary of each other, open conflict has never surfaced. We have always co-existed, why now?"

"You have been away for many years, my friend," Masintet explained gesticulating with his hands to drive the point home. "During that period you were away, people invaded forests, cut down trees, cleared the undergrowth and turned thousands of acres into farmlands. The trees that were not suitable for timber were not spared either. They have been stripped of their barks and they now look like ghostly skeletons. Their only use before they are cut down for charcoal is to provide perching points for flocks of angry staring crows."

"What sections of the forest are you talking about?" asked Kedoki, concerned.

"The entire forest!" said Mansintet. "None has been spared. They include Shapa-iltarakwa, Ololturoto, Ilbaoi, Sasimuani, Sikinterr and even Medungi,"

"They destroyed even Medungi? "Kedoki asked bewildered.

"Yes, they fell giant trees in Medungi forest," Masintet said sadly. "I believe that is the reason why animals who have been largely harmless, have suddenly become vicious."

Kedoki retreated into a contemplative mood. His mind raced back in time, to the only time he and his friends ventured into Medungi forest. They were hot in pursuit of cattle rustlers who had stolen ten of his steers. When the trail led them to Medungi forest, they stopped and debated among themselves as to the wisdom of entering the sacred forest that the ancestors forbid any interaction with whatsoever. To scare the dare-devils who were wont to trying anything forbidden, the *loibon* said that if a tree was cut in that forest, it would bleed profusely and the rest of the trees would wail and scream like tormented human beings. The blood of the felled trees would flow to the rivers, turn them red and poison man and beast. When Kedoki and his friends thought of what might befall them if they entered into the forbidden forest and accidentally broke a twig of the sacred trees, they got scared and shied away. They took a detour and found a different route. Kedoki and his party of brave men called *enkitungat* combed other dense forests, time and again, in pursuit of either cattle rustlers or menacing animals. In all those occasions, not once did they find a single reason to cut down a tree. Nor did anyone else, for that matter.

He felt sad and angry when he thought that the evergreen *Shapa – Iltarakwa* trees that preferred the south-facing slopes, rich with loamy soils and sufficient rains were no more.

He recalled once, when he entered Ilpoldon dense forest, near Olpusi-moru where huge podo trees that soared to over a hundred feet in the sky grew on the lower part of Oloolongoi slopes. They blended perfectly into thick clusters of golden colour bamboo whose hollow segmented stems towered above all other trees and seemed to reach the height of the podo trees. In stark reality, they were shorter for they grew on the higher part of the escarpment. In addition, tall stands of giant *ilourrurr* trees also climbed to over a hundred feet, above the undergrowth.

On the other side of the Mau forest, where the tilt of the hills faced west and where the soils were ever moist and fertile, hardwood, cedars such as *olpiripiri*, *oltarakuai*, and many others, attained amazing heights. Immense sacred and holy trees such as *olngaboli*, *oreteti*, *oseki* and *oloirien* – that intertwined with *olpalagilagi* and *olosiro* undergrowth, crowded the forest, making it nearly impenetrable.

On Oloshepani slanted hillsides, where the breaks in the leafy canopy allowed more sunlight to reach the ground, the undergrowth was often luxuriant, with flowering *oloiramirami* and *olkilenyai* climbers trailing down from the high branches of the canopy. It was in that forest that he often saw a variety of birds species making their nests, and in the warmer season of the year found the *olkinyei* woods alive with breeding *ilekishu* birds, nestling in every conceivable crany. Hyraxes screeched sorrowfully, colobus monkeys, with black and white fur on their skins, jumped long distances, from tree to tree, their high pitch grunts filling the air.

He recalled sorrowfully how he and his late brother discovered a bee tree. With the help of a smoky torch, his brother climbed using an improvised ladder made from the fallen trunk of a tree with stumps of sturdy branches still attached to it, braved a few stings from the bees to collect some honeycombs. They merrily gobbled up the sweet rare treat, eating the *ilchankaro* honeycomb with a few milky crunchy larvae. They laughed like children at the sticky mess they made of themselves.

The forests were always full of life. It was home to many animals and birds. It was also home for *Olkiek* people who were then called *Iltorrobo*. It was a place of refuge where man and beast ran to at times of trouble or danger. Sometimes, although he walked all day and saw no animal, he knew with certainty that he walked within a few metres of many creatures. The animals would have heard and smelt him and perhaps seen him, without him even suspecting their presence. In a mysterious way, whenever he was in the forest, he felt as if he was being watched all the time by anxious eyes. In turn, he was always on the look out, peering down each glade, turning his head and flicking his eyes to catch the first sight of a pair of horns and pricked ears, the flash of a retreating rump, the whisk of a tail and the silent vanishing of an animal into the bush or forest. The whole landscape was full of life and he felt part of it. Curiously, the absence of human beings in the forest made it more exciting and momentous. He never felt lonely, although now and then he was exposed to real danger.

He recalled one time when they went for an *olamaiyo*, which was the hunt for a menacing animal. The purpose was to hunt down a lion that had killed a neighbour's ox. They were ten young men and each wore his short *shuka*, headgear of ostrich plumes, carried a long spear and an oval-shaped shield made of tough buffalo hide. They chased the lion which disappeared into the forest. It got into a thicket which they ringed. They then provoked it by throwing sticks at it. Suddenly it charged out of the thicket, and tried to break the circle that the young men had made. One of them threw a spear at it wounding it. It growled and snarled angrily and once more charged out of the circle, striking one of the young men dead as it bounded past, only for it to fall, with its hide full of spears that stuck out of it like quills on a dead porcupine. At the end of it all, man and beast lay side by side dead in the forest. None of them could, nevertheless claim an overriding right of ownership of the forest.

Norpisia stared at Masintet while he talked. His words had put her mind into a spin. The terrifying dream that she had had a few days before Masintet and Lembarta arrived, returned to haunt her. Of late, she had been in a mood to communicate with her grandmother through the spiritual world, she thought that would explain the strange state of mind she was in. With untold bewilderment, she thought it was almost too coincidental that she would dream of her grandmother urgently urging her to run to the hills in the highland and join wild animals to fight a multi-headed monster that had invaded the forests and then, just a few days later a man would walk into the wilderness and talk of animals ganging up to fight human beings who destroyed the animals habitat as well as impeding their God-given freedom of movement in search of pasture. Was that the answer to her dream?

She pondered why man would want to destroy the animals' habitat and in so doing destroy human life as well. She knew God had given humans and animals a chance to co-exist, every species minding its own business. She recalled the time they were crossing the vast grassland, driving their herd of cattle and flock of sheep and goats. One particular day in a sunny afternoon, she and Kedoki stopped at the top of a high hill within the central area that ran parallel to a river. A vast panoramic view commanded their direction. Except for the faint grey shapes of the Mau escarpments to the west, the expansive vista was uninterrupted. And for all its uniformity, the savannah land with its green vegetation rippling in the gentle wind, was deceptively rich. On it, she saw large and small animals graze side by side peacefully. As it was on the grasslands, so was it in the forests where buffaloes, warthogs, wild pigs and other forest inhabitants co-existed with the Olkiek and the Ndorobo, with none pushing the other to extinction.

She had asked Kedoki why nature introduced predators to disturb such serene tranquility. He had explained to her how the tremendous herds of grazers as well as the browsers had to be culled and their numbers kept in check from time to time by the carnivores. Lions, hyenas, leopards, wild dogs and foxes had to adapt to the environment in which their prey lived so as to ensure a constant supply of their food. They, therefore, hunted the sick, the young, the old and the wounded ensuring that only the fittest of them survived. In so doing, nature ensured that there was a sustainable number of every species in the savanna and in the forests.

Watching animals life in the savannah, Norpisia realized that each species had to struggle to survive in their natural habitat. Therefore, human interference with the natural habitat could only meddle with animal's life and make it much more difficult for them to survive.

She recalled one sunny morning when she stood on a small hill and watched with trepidation as a leopard stalked two reed-bucks playing on a small knoll not far from where she stood. The leopard crawled stealthily, inch by inch, in the tall grass. Oblivious of the looming danger, the two bucks carried on with their play. With his outstretched neck, the buck bounded after the doe and at some unseen signal, the male whipped round and fled and in turn, the smaller doe ran after him. They leapt with the grace and freedom of the wind, their slender feet and ankles firm and strong, precisely stepping where they intended without faltering. The leopard inched closer and Norpisia felt like shouting to alert the two reedbucks of the danger, but she dared not. Norpisia sighed with relief when some warning from the wind halted their game. They stood for an instant, frozen by alarm and then with a shrill sharp whistle, bounded for shelter and vanished into the bush. The leopard thoroughly frustrated by its inability to make a kill snarled hungrily then turned and walked sluggishly away.

Norpisia had watched pleasantly the expansive grassland that was teeming with all kinds of animals that spread to the horizon. The variety of colours of their herd of black, white, red and grey cattle, their goats and sheep, made the savannah a mosaic of all colours, so pleasing to the eye. She was saddened by the fact that humans, by cutting down trees in the forest and clearing the undergrowth, were on the verge of dispossessing animals of their habitat. It was what she had observed many times among all creatures inhabiting those hills, plains and forests, from ostriches to the dung-beetles, and from wildebeests to the hares. It was all routine as all the creatures ventured forth at dawn in search of food. As the morning light spread, the browsing, the scurring, fluttering about, the flash of various colours in dappled sunlight, filled the air. Then in the afternoon, when the sun was hot, there was a falling tempo when grazing and browsing were suspended. There followed a tail-twitching doze, of drowsing under tree branches, and later in the evening, a gradual renewal of life as grazing was resumed. As night approached, there was slumber for one set of living creatures while another set came to life to fill their bellies under the stars. It was a scene of restlessness, of unremitting activities devoted to the purpose of keeping alive.

When she eventually stretched herself on the hard ground to sleep, her mind churned haphazardly, bringing forth disjointed dreams. Her grandmother surfaced and pointed at her scolding, accusing her of not obeying her instructions to go to the forest in the highlands and join the animals to fight the forest invaders. Then, the human and animal conflict was re-played. She saw men with spears facing a combined force of angry elephants, rhinos, buffaloes, giraffes, wildebeest, zebras, elands, lions, leopards, cheetahs and many other animals that stood their ground, declaring that they had as much right to the forest, just as man did. The stand off continued for a very long time. Just then, Kedoki was wounded, not by the animals, but by his fellow men. Seeing him writhing in pain, brought the sad dream to an abrupt end.

She woke up trembling and sweating profusely. What did the dream portend? Was it a pointer to a forthcoming incident? She fearfully searched her mind, though no answer was forthcoming.

CHAPTER 7

Over the next few weeks, the four, Kedoki, Masintet, Lembarta and Norpisia were on the move, with their herd, toward the eastern ridges of the Mau forest. They left behind the olive-green woods of the lower slopes and entered into a wild terrain with a thick, dark forest. It thrust down to the plains that were dotted with thorn bushes and creased by gullies. Occasionally, a strong wind blew from the highlands, across the sky that was heavily laden with pregnant clouds. They threatened a deluge, at any time.

The three men ensured that their herd grazed uninterrupted. Kedoki led the animals, controlling their movement by turning back those that rushed ahead of the rest, while Masintet and Lembarta flanked them, ensuring that none went astray.

Norpisia brought up the rear, occasionally combing the bushes thoroughly to ensure that no kid, lamb or calf was left behind. When the animals slowed down and began to graze contentedly, each man stood stock-still like a flamingo bird, leaning on his spear, a leg hoisted up so that his foot rested on the knee of the other leg. In this position, they sent a constant predatory gaze all around the cattle, to ensure that at no time were they caught unaware by the ever present attackers who hid in the forest.

Norpisia loved the sound of cowbells and goatbells, more so, when it emanated from the bells that dangled down the necks of their cows and goats. It was music to her ears, it helped to break the monotonous silence of the forest. She also loved the dry smell of goats mingled with the aromatic smell of *olokuai* shrub, and the scent of leaf-mould that blended with a whiff of sweet aroma of *esongoyo* creepers. Those familiar smells were ever present in her grandmother's homestead. They were part of nature's book from which she learned its pervasive wonders. It was from that same book that her grandmother taught her the truth and beauty found in every bush, tree, stream and river.

It was, therefore, with an open mind that she ventured into the forest where she found herself walking through a tangle of spiky under-growth that grew under the huge-trunked sweet-scented cedar trees. The trees were so tall that they tapered off to the sky with grey moss hanging from their twisted branches overhead. They looked like old bearded giant men. The inside of the forest was dark, moist and at first silent. But after a while, Norpisia became aware of various muted sounds. For instance, she identified the rustling sounds of chewing insects, the stirring of leaves, the burrowing of small creatures and the quiet flight of birds. Sometimes, she caught a glimpse of colobus monkeys, with their brilliant white and black skins, leaping from branch to branch overhead.

The part of Mau forest they were traversing had not been inhabited save for the *iltorrobo* who moved within and through it in search of honey. They saw no *ilmuaten* or relics of abandoned homesteads. It was apparent that no human hand had ever cut a tree in that forest or dug gardens in those glades.

Suddenly, Norpisia felt apprehensive. The atmosphere had become eerie and weird. There seemed to be a presence in that forest, a spirit or something that was almost sentient. It was causing goose-pimples to rise in her body. What was it? She wondered fearfully.

At that time, Kedoki was leading the herd out of the forest to a short plain that sloped to a river where he intended to water them. He suddenly stiffened with apprehension when he saw one of the three dogs that were following him, break away from the rest and race towards a thicket of acacia, barking, and snarling. He gripped his spear firmly and ready to face any eventuality. Suddenly, he heard a thud, and the dog squealed in agony as it fell to the ground. He immediately knew they were under attack from *ilainyamok*, the beastly cattle rustlers. A ripple passed through the sheep and goats and they were suddenly in a headlong run toward the river, followed by the cattle that bellowed in panic.

Kedoki froze for an instant when he saw a tall man, a spear raised high above his head, springing toward him. When he gathered strength, he too raised his spear and the two adversaries faced off, each ready to hurl a deadly spear into the other's rib-cage. The cattle rustler was swift and stalked Kedoki before he saw him. He was, therefore, ready for the attack long before Kedoki knew he was being stalked. He hurled his spear at Kedoki expertly stabbing him at the thigh, thus pinning him down onto the ground. Kedoki fell, dropped all his weapons as he grabbed his bleeding leg with both his hands. As he writhed in pain, his first thought was not about his herd but on Norpisia. How he hoped the beast would not harm her.

"Oiye atara!" he yelled painfully, trying to attract the attention of Masintet and Lembarta.

Little did Kedoki know that his two companions were at that time engaged in their own fierce battle. None of them had any idea that rustlers had staged a fork attack after their morning reconnaissance had informed them that there were three herders driving a large herd of cattle and flocks of sheep and goats. Once they had assessed their strength, each of them was assigned to attack one herder, while the fourth was to drive away a number of cattle. Luckily they did not see Norpisia, or if they did, they ignored her, possibly dismissing her as a harmless woman.

For a moment, the pain in Kedoki's leg was moderated by the shock of the sudden attack that resulted in immense loss of blood that caused numbness on the left side of his body. At last, the pain descended upon him in seething waves which centered in his thigh and raced through his entire body. He could not move an inch for the spear that still underpinned him onto the ground was razor sharp and any movement he made tore into his flesh farther.

"Oh God, please see to it that they do not molest Norpisia," he cried deliriously.

He dug his elbows into the ground and tried to lift himself up to look at his leg. The pain intensified as the spear tore into his flesh. He winced and gasped while bracing his elbows and lifted himself a little higher. He clenched his muscles in his left leg to move his foot. The pain became excruciating, but his foot moved a little. His arms suddenly became weak and he stiffened them with an effort and turned his head to scan the slope, searching to see whether he could locate the rustler who had speared him. He knew he would certainly come back for his spear. And he reckoned that would be the end of his life. But if the rustler found him alive, he would pierce him to death. What then would happen to Norpisia? He sagged back to the ground panting painfully.

The fact that he would lose all his cattle, sheep and goats to the rustlers was devastatingly painful. But equally painful was the feeling that most likely, Masintet and Lembarta were already dead. His greatest fear, however, was what the bestial brutes would do to Norpisia when they caught up with her. They would probably molest, rape and possibly abduct her. He was chocked by a galling anger, decrying the fact that his life-long struggle and sweat, his beloved Norpisia, were all to be taken away by the bandits who preyed on others' livestock. He too was angry at himself for his failure to be watchful.

The time he had laid there in the dappled shade of a tree seemed to him to be an eternity. The rich smell of the decaying leaves in the soil was strong in his nostrils. And the ground was soft and cool against the side of his face. However, the longer he lay helplessly, the more his strength ebbed. His leg was bleeding badly and he feared that it would not be long before his strength deserted him entirely, taking away his consciousness.

Then, what he feared most happened. Four white-breasted vultures flashed through the air and perched in a nearby bush. He knew the predatory birds were attracted by the smell of his blood. If he lost consciousness, even for a minute, they would immediately poke out his eyes before disembowelling him mercilessly. They fluttered their wings rapidly and then landed a few metres from where he lay. He looked absentmindedly at their hooked beaks, strong talons and hawky bead-like eyes that darted from side to side as they surveyed him and the area.

He cringed fearfully. An overwhelming apprehensive mood seized him, stiffening his body. His eyes dilated and the saliva in his mouth dried up. He thought he detected a movement in the trees as a couple of leaves on the lower branch of a tree stirred slightly. A swift shadow flicked from one tree to another in the space of time it took an eye to blink. His eyes were riveted on the tree and he nearly missed another movement.

On the other side, near the bush from where the

cattle rustler had earlier emerged, he saw two men, each holding a drawn sword, crawling stealthily toward him. His end had finally come, he told himself despairingly. Just then, he saw Norpisia! Her slim body stretched out along the ground under a low branch in the bush. In her right hand she held his late brother's spear, in her left hand a bow and two arrows. A quiver dangled down from her shoulders. She was completely motionless and invisible against the mottled pattern of the ground and the foliage. He turned, looked at the approaching men and then back to Norpisia. It was then that he realized that she had seen the two men. She was stalking them! He was gripped by an uncontrollable fear. How could he warn her to stop her foolishness? What could a young woman do when pitted against two hardened cattle rustlers? How could he warn her to retreat without alerting the beastly brutes? Who could tell her that she was nothing but a small thin woman, thinking she could face two armed men? He was troubled.

Suddenly, he saw Norpisia dart across the open space in the forest. Her first step was a full stride in a headlong dash at the crawling men. She was halfway across the open space before Kedoki's mind figured out what his eyes were seeing. She was running fast, her slender body bowed backward with her right arm raised high above her head, the muscles in it knotted, as she firmly held her spear. Her eyes were wide open and her lips drawn back from her teeth in an expression of wild fury. She hurled her spear, which forcefully flew through the air toward one of the two men. The tall man, who Kedoki recognized as the one who wounded him, glimpsed at her belatedly and raised his sword as he quickly got up to face her. The sharp end of Norpisia's spear pierced into him, sending him sprawling, blood gushing out of his rib-cage like crimson water from a fountain. Before the other man could attack her, Norpisia had shot an arrow at him. The arrow got him squarely between his shoulder blades. The man yelled as he fell backward, fatally wounded.

She then dashed to where Kedoki lay, grinning, her bared teeth gleaming in the bright afternoon's sunshine. He noticed that she was trembling.

Just then, Masintet and Lembarta arrived. They immediately got hold of Norpisia and wrestled her to the ground. They held her there forcefully as she jerked and writhed. Foam oozed from her mouth and her eyes dilated and turned white as they rolled in their sockets. She gnashed her teeth and deliriously called out the names of her grandmother, her dead sister and her dead brother. Slowly the spasm eased and her body went limp.

It was then that the two brothers turned to Kedoki. They lifted him together with the spear in his thigh and slowly laid him on the green grass under the shade of a tree.

Masintet was a junior elder who, during the eight years he was a moran, faced all kinds of danger and had become an expert in dealing with emergencies like the one facing them. He sent his brother into the bush to look for *enabooi* herb while he debated within himself on how best to pull the spear out of Kedoki's flesh without inflicting more injuries. Kedoki was patient and courageous. He bore the excruciating pain stoically.

Soon, Lembarta returned with an ample supply of succulent stems of *enabooi* plant. He was instructed to beat them into pulp. Masintet instructed him to hold the wet soft lump in his hand, ready to stuff it into the gaping hole that would be left in Kedoki's thigh when he pulled out the spear. Kedoki grimaced in anticipated pain, for he knew what Masintet was about to do. He too had done that for other injured men several times in the past. Masintet stepped on Kedoki's shoulder and forcefully yanked the spear out of his flesh. Kedoki screamed and groaned in pain as fresh blood gushed out of the wound. Lembarta then stuffed the pulp into the gaping wound, immediately reducing the flow of blood. Masintet tore a piece of his *shuka* and bandaged the injured leg. By the time they were through with the messy operation, the thick blood in their hands made them nauseous.

"The beasts have paid this with their lives," Masintet said angrily. "You are certainly brave. You have single-handedly managed to kill the two armed brutes."

"I didn't kill them," Kedoki said haltingly as he writhed in pain. "I was caught unaware and was speared before I could hit back."

Masintet and Lembarta exchanged puzzled gazes.

"Who did this then?" a puzzled Masintet asked, pointing at the bodies of the two dead men.

"It was Norpisia who did it," Kedoki said proudly, even as he groaned in pain. "She has saved my life!"

"What a brave woman!" exclaimed Masintet. "*Taba*!"

"Only *Enkaikipiani* can manage such a feat!" Lembarta commented enthusiastically. "I would say with certainty that this is not a woman but a man!"

"I hope the brutes have left a few heads of cattle to enable us rekindle the fire," Kedoki said weakly as his mind refused to contemplate life without his cattle. "And to think that the bastards coolly drove them away without allowing me the slightest chance to fight back and defend my god-given inheritance!"

"*Intirringayu*!" Masintet called sharply. "Relax man, relax."

"What is a man without his cattle?" the agitated Kedoki groaned distressfully. He was overwhelmed by what he visualized to be the irrecoverable loss of all that he had valued in his life.

Kedoki could not believe Masintet's words when he told him that he and his brother Lembarta had fought the cattle rustlers killing one of them. They also informed him that they then pursued one rustler who swiftly drove fifty heads of cattle through the forest, caught up with him and recovered the cattle. Although he managed to escape, he left behind a trail of blood, indicating that he would not survive.

They drove back the fifty heads of cattle into the herd, which was now intact, without a single loss. Kedoki was overwhelmingly delighted and could not thank the two men sufficiently.

When Norpisia regained her composure and after comprehending the state of her husband's injury, she hugged him, praising God for having spared his life.

Eventually, when all of them had come to terms with the situation, they re-organized their strategies. Lembarta went to drive the cattle down the river after they had lifted Kedoki and placed him onto a donkey. They slowly carried him to the place where they were to stop for the night. Norpisia made her *olngoborr*, while Masintet and Lembarta constructed the thorn-fenced cattle enclosure.

With the sun shining behind the rolling black clouds, discolouring them to a livid red and purple, the evening cooled off quickly in the wooded valley where their camp was situated. As Norpisia waited for the pot of soup she was preparing for Kedoki to boil, she sat in the last glow of twilight, contemplating the sickening events of the day. She recalled the eerie feeling that had overwhelmed her in the forest that afternoon just before the cattle rustlers struck. The fear reminded her of that time when bandits struck her home, killing her brother and sister before driving away her father's livestock.

The fact that they had not driven far away from the scene of the attack, troubled Norpisia. Although she had killed two of the rustlers, and Lembarta and Masintet killed the other, and probably only one of them escaped injured, she thought the one who escaped could survive and bring back other attackers to avenge their dead comrades. This made her uneasy, and the feeling worsened with the coming of the night. Beside those frightening thoughts, she was also feeling a bit unwell, suffering from a slight headache and backache. She attributed her disquiet to the slight discomforts she occasionally experienced when her body ovulated.

That night, she slept next to Kedoki as she attended to his high fever. And as she lay close to him, she listened to the wind moaning as it sighed through the swaying cedar trees, silhouetted against silvery clouds. The glowing full moon, encircled by a distinct halo, took turns hiding behind it, then brilliantly illuminating the softly textured sky.

Kedoki was aware that he lay next to the fire near *olngoborr*. His mind floated drowsily in and out of consciousness. There were urgent concerns that gnawed at him, but they seemed very distant. Once in a while, his surroundings intruded, making sound and movement register in his awareness. He opened his eyes and recognized Norpisia lying next to him. He struggled to sit up. He then held her with both hands clasping her shoulders, as she lay on her back. He looked into her eyes with a fierce determination, seeking reassurance that she understood him clearly.

She saw his conviction and his love. Kedoki looked down at her, watching her breath peacefully, loving the sight of her full, womanly form, and delighting in the knowledge that she loved him.

"Recovering my cattle and knowing that my woman loves me," he said resolutely, "makes me want to live to fight another day!"

CHAPTER 8

Norpisia woke up several times at night to check on Kedoki. He had had a fitful sleep, frequently interrupted by disturbing nightmares. The pain in his thigh came in waves, swelling to a wracking intensity and subsiding again. Intermittently, distorted images moved about him at times and at other times there was only a cold and lonely darkness. He shivered and at the same time sweated with fever. When he suddenly shot up to a sitting position, she held onto his arm, persuading him to lie down and soothingly lulled him to sleep. It didn't take long before he was at it again. Terror gripped him after his tortured mind took him back to the events of the previous day. Several times, he asked Norpisia to bring him water to drink. And when she did, he drank very little saying the water was musty and bitter.

Norpisia's eyes were open as the first morning glow crept in through the smoke hole of the *olngoborr* and sent its faint illuminating rays into the folds of the hide and skins that made up the walls of the *olngoborr*. It dispersed the darkness and brought the hidden shapes out of the concealing shadows. By the time the obscurity of the night had retreated to a dim half light, she was already wide awake and could not go back to sleep.

Moving quickly away from Kedoki's warmth, she got up and took a calabash from a rack where she placed other calabashes and then slipped outside the *olngoborr*. The night chill enveloped her bare skin and the cold wind that blew from the hills clothed her with goose pimples. Looking out across the misty valley, she saw the vague formation of the still unlit landscape on the opposite side of the forest, silhouetted against the glowing sky. She wished they were already out of that dreadful location. Shivering, she walked through the cattle enclosure where cattle, sheep and goats rested peacefully. Outside the kraal, she walked through the damp grass that was dripping wet with dew, towards a small narrow stream that flowed between giant trees. As she walked, she sensed the rising of the sun in the east. She observed the eastern sky shade from glowing grey to soft-blue, with a scattering of pink clouds, reflecting the glory of the morning sun. She watched the slowly changing patterns with wonder, held by the magnificence of the back side of the sunrise.

By the time she reached the little stream of clean clear water that raced and skipped down the slope, the morning chill had burned off. She filled the calabash at the splashing cascade that ran into the slight depression of the pool, then climbed out of the river bank. She then took a detour and got into the forest searching for herbs. Her grandmother, who was a renowned medicine-woman, had imparted to her a great deal of valuable knowledge of various kinds of herbs. She searched for herbs that she would use to treat the swelling on Kedoki's leg. She found *olmasiligi* with its thick large succulent leaves, uprooted several whole plant that she was to heat over the fire. She would place the hot, fleshy leaves on the swollen part of his leg. She would also boil the whole plant to make a wash, for it contained skin-healing and wound-suppurating curatives.

When she saw the tiny leaves of *olmagiro-ngiro*, she picked them to add to the solution. She knew they were excellent for healing anything from bites to boils, even severe ulcers and wounds. Further out of the forest where it was dryer, she dug out roots of *olkonyil* to add to his soup as a general antidote for poisons and other toxic reactions. They already had *olkitolosua* roots that they often added to their soup to help boost energy and warm their bodies.

She was quite pleased to find the bright green leaves of *olosesiate* which she valued most for their antiseptic and quick-healing properties. They were also effective in keeping flies away from a wound. She would pound them and make a strong solution that she would often splash on Kedoki's wound.

Growing at the sunny edges of the woods, she found *olcani-lenkashe* herb, which was not only a good fly-repellent when made into an infusion for an external wash, but an excellent addition to the soup that made a person sweat profusely and helped to open up pores on the skin. She then dug up tubers and collected twigs, berries and barks of trees and carried them all to their temporary camp.

In the afternoon, Kedoki watched her as she prepared the herbs. He asked her many questions and listened to her explanations with interest. He felt lucky to be with a woman who knew so much about herbal medicine. In less than a week, he was on his way to full recuperation.

Masintet and Lembarta were not satisfied with the location of the temporary camp. It was right inside the forest and therefore vulnerable to attacks from wild animals and cattle rustlers. Norpisia felt the same. Since that afternoon when they were attacked by the cattle rustlers, she always felt uneasy. Kedoki also felt a great desire to protect her. Now that he was not in a position to physically protect her, he thought relocation was the best security measure.

There was a consensus by all, that they should move to a more open area. Kedoki had not yet regained full strength and they could not, therefore, travel very far from where they were. After crossing a number of streams, they eventually found a suitable place to camp. The place was on a clear hillside, with no trees. As Norpisia erected her *olngoborr*, Masintet and Lembarta cut thorn-bushes and dragged them to the site to make the cattle enclosure.

Kedoki rested under an acacia bush with birds chirruping on top as they weaved their nests. Soon, everyone, except Kedoki, was busy collecting firewood. Although the sun still stood some way above the horizon, it was already cold enough for them to need a fire. Within no time, a fire was blazing and on it a chunk of mutton was sizzling; drops of fat igniting the flames.

When the mutton was ready, it was equally shared among the four of them. Norpisia silently chewed her share admiring the view that the hill on which they camped commanded. Ahead on that hill, the land stretched forever into the setting sun that was inflaming the whole sky with purple, crimson and gold. The scenery rekindled in her memories of her home at Olomuruti. She was filled with nostalgia. She wondered why such a sight should always sadden her. To distract the feeling, she stood up, collected a calabash from within the *olngoborr* and walked slowly to a nearby stream to fetch water.

On her way back, she was overwhelmed by the beautiful scenery that stretched to the horizon before her eyes. Thousands upon thousands of wild animals were grazing on the bluish green tall grass that rippled in waves like the sea. In the sky, she saw a soaring *olkupelia* bird seeking a nibbling shrew. She heard crickets trill in the nearby bushes. She knew hyraxes drowsed in the hollow of the trees in the forest and on the same trees perched the ugly vultures with their almost featherless heads and necks, waiting to find another dying animal. She marvelled at the symbiotic relationship of nature. Sadly, she thought, only human beings played a destructive role in that cycle of life. Only human beings, she concluded, were not content to leave things as nature had intended them to be. Even when they changed them, she thought angrily, they were seldom satisfied with the result.

Later that night after Lembarta and Masintet had

gone to keep their nightly vigil, Norpisia reminded Kedoki of the dreams that she once had and which partly came true.

"I once told you about a dream I had," she told him as she reached over to a pile of firewood for a stick, uncovered hot coals in the bed of ashes and then tossed bits of bark on them. The fire burst into flames and she tossed more pieces of wood into it. She moved closer to sit near it. "In that dream, I called you, but you faded away leaving me standing there desperately."

"Yes, you told me," Kedoki answered quietly. "As I told you then, it was a dream. We must leave it as such."

"No, my husband," she protested mildly. "A dream stops being a dream when it comes true."

"It could have been just a coincidence," he said nonchalantly. "Nothing more than that."

She tried to argue her case about the dreams but he seemed adamant and did not understand what she meant about them. Or if he did, he did not take her seriously. The dreams, however, kept on disturbing her mind. She recalled the first dream where she saw a giant lion crash into their cattle enclosure and pounce on a heifer. In the dream, Kedoki came out holding his spear to face the ferocious animal then, everything became hazy and Kedoki began to fade away. She called him desperately, but he did not answer her. Then, she recalled the other dream where Kedoki was injured, not by animals, but by his fellow human beings. Most disturbing were the last parts of the two dreams where her grandmother appeared, urging her to go to the forest in the highlands and help wild animals fight a multi-headed monster that had invaded the forest.

Although Kedoki treated her explanation of the dreams with nonchalance, she believed recent events lent credence to them. When Masintet arrived and narrated to her how angry animals were fighting back human beings for having destroyed their habitats, she did not require a better explanation to tell her the dreams were becoming a reality. And when the cattle rustlers attacked, she linked the incident to the second dream. But when she thought of that night when Kedoki sat on a stone near the fire in their *olngoborr*, with his head drooping, fighting giddiness and unconsciousness, she wondered whether it was a pointer that he was going to die soon, leaving her lonely and without his child. She certainly needed his son to inherit his name and cattle.

They were sitting close to the fire drinking the hot soup she had prepared. One of the dogs that Norpisia liked had hovered close to her all evening but now he seemed content to curl up near her feet when she sat near the warm fire. She picked the oblong piece of hide that she had been working on the whole day and began shaping it with her knife.

"What are you making?" Kedoki asked.

"An *olchuret*." She paused for a moment as she straightened it with her hands. "It's a head covering to shield you from the rain. It may rain heavily soon and I thought you might require it."

"How did you know I might require an *olchuret* even before the onset of the rains?"

"A caring wife learns to anticipate the needs of her husband," she said smilingly.

"Without doubt, you are my beloved wife," he answered, smiling back at her. "And I certainly will announce it to the whole village at Nkararo the moment we arrive. But all the same, how do you anticipate the needs of someone else without them telling you what they want?"

"It is not difficult," she said excitedly. "You just think about situations that might make their life comfortable." After a moment of silence she added.

"A woman must anticipate a man's needs. Since he protects her and her children from danger. Who would protect them if anything were to happen to him?"

"Is that what you are doing?" he asked while grinning mischievously, "protecting me now so that I will protect you and your children in the future?"

"Well, not exactly," she answered quietly as she concentrated her look on the dying embers, "I think it's the way a wife tells her husband how much she loves him and cares for him, whether she has children or not but I think I need to tell you I want to have your child before I get too old."

"You have a long way to go," he said jokingly as he put another piece of wood on the fire. "You are still very young."

"No, I'm getting to be an old woman," she said seriously, closing her eyes to concentrate on what she was saying. "Women of my age back at Olomuruti are already getting their second child."

"I should be the one complaining," he said lightheartedly. "But I am not. You are strong and healthy. When the time comes for you to have children, you will have as many as you wish. But let me tell you something, Norpisia. You amaze me with how much you know! Frankly, there are times I look at your eyes and they seem ancient, as though you have experienced so much in your short life."

Norpisia stopped her work for a while and looked at him straight in the eyes. It was unusual for him to make such a comment. He too looked at her and their eyes locked. The feeling she evoked in him was almost frightening. She was so beautiful in the light of the fire, and he loved her so much, he didn't know what he would do if anything ever happened to her. He thought of how she recently saved his life, and she was now nursing him back to good health and a constriction rose in his throat. Tears also welled in his eyes. Overcame with emotion, he looked away. Then, to ease the moment, he tried to introduce a lighter subject.

"I'm the one who should worry about age," he said laughing uproariously. "When we eventually get to my village at Nkararo, you will find out that men of my age-group got married ages ago and they are all settled with three or four wives and many children." *"Norpisia-ai-nanyorr,"* he called her fondly, "I want you to have a child too, but not while we are travelling through the

92

wilderness. Not until we are safely back at Nkararo, my village, and you are in your own house, not in an *olngoborr*."

As she finished sewing the head straps on the *olchuret* she felt the soft sprinkling of rain. She hurried out to bring everything that was outside into the *olngoborr*. Later at night, as she lay on the hard ground, she felt anxious and achy, but she tried not to toss and turn too much so that she didn't disturb Kedoki. She listened to the pattering of the rain on the hides that roofed the *olngoborr*, but the rain did not lull her to sleep the way it usually did. She remained awake thinking of their discussion that evening about children. Finally she slept soundly.

She was woken up by grunts of a wildebeest that was being chased by a pack of hyenas outside the cattle enclosure. She quickly got out of the *olngoborr* in pitch darkness and collected a few stones from the ground. She threw them at the hyenas to drive them away from near the cattle enclosure. One of the hyenas whooped, then several others cackled a loud laugh that made Norpisia's skin crawl. Knowing that it was not easy for hyenas to kill a healthy wildebeest, she wondered whether the wildebeest that was being hunted down was sick or probably trapped in a snare laid by poachers.

When the noise faded away she walked back to the *olngoborr*. She had just gotten beneath the blanket when Kedoki rolled over and she turned to listen to the man she loved lying beside her, breathing with the deep rhythms of sleep. She was afraid that if she moved she would wake him up and she hated to disturb him, especially then when he was recovering from the injury on his leg. She remained still for quite sometime, but when she later moved slowly, trying to ease out of the warm, slightly damp blanket, he snorted, and rolled over. It was when he reached for her and found her missing that he woke up.

"Norpisia-ai, where are you?" he mumbled,

"Go back to sleep," she told him soothingly as she crawled out of the *olngoborr*, "you don't have to get up yet."

CHAPTER 9

Six months after he was wounded, after devouring meat from six healthy he-goats and taking mugfuls of soup laced with Norpisia's herbs, Kedoki recovered well enough to propose the resumption of their journey. He did not immediately tell Norpisia about his suggestion, but she noticed that he was troubled. He held several discussions with Masintet and Lembarta privately. At first, it did not bother her. She thought it was normal for men to discuss among themselves, matters they thought did not concern women. But he often seemed distracted and for the past several days he went about his business with a look of anxious concern on his face. She began to get concerned.

"Something seems to be bothering you of late," she told him as they sat outside the *olngoborr* watching the sun set.

Kedoki turned to look at the distant hills to the west that were illuminated by the dying rays of the setting sun. He wished the distant hills would tell him what lay ahead and whether he was making the right decision! If it were just his brother, his sister and himself travelling, it didn't matter too much. Such a journey would be in pursuit of pasture and adventure. Whatever else that came along became part of their normal pastoralists' nomadic life.

This return journey was different. He was travelling back home without his brother and sister and more so, he was with a woman he loved more than life itself. Not only did he want to take her to Nkararo, but he also wanted to get her there safely. He wanted to show her off, as a man who had gone to a great battle and triumphed, would return home to show off the cattle he brought back. The more he thought about the possible dangers they might encounter along the way, the more he imagined even greater ones. What troubled him most was that, his vague worries were not something he could easily explain to Norpisia.

"I am just worried about how long our journey through Olpurkel will take," he said concerned. "We need to cross the Enkipai river before it floods, otherwise we are doomed."

"You have told me that before," she said puzzled. "But why do you say we are doomed if we don't cross it by then? And why should we worry about going through Olpurkel when we have not yet crossed the treacherous Osupuko?"

"When that river is flooded, it presents the greatest challenge to any herdsman," he explained, with a serious concerned tone evident in his deep voice. "The swollen river flows so swiftly that it becomes too dangerous to cross. Moreover, that is the time numerous herds of wildebeests, zebras and elands also choose to cross the river in pursuit of fresh green pastures."

"I suppose there are many places along the river where it is safe to cross," Norpisia pursued the subject relentlessly. "Why then would the crossing of wildebeests, zebras and other wild animals be of any concern to us?"

"Because opportunistic predators converge at the river-crossings ready to pounce on easy prey," explained Kedoki explicitly. "Lions, hyenas, wild dogs and crocodiles stay at the edge of the river ready to pull out exhausted animals that struggle to cross against a swift strong current. If your herd is crossing at that time, it suffers the same fate as that of wild animals. To make the situation worse, many of our cows will be calving down soon. Young calves may not make it across the river."

"Well, if it is that dangerous, then we won't attempt to cross the river," she said as a matter of fact, then she asked, "But if we can't cross the river in time, what do we do then? Is there any other way around the problem?"

"I'm not very sure of an alternative," Kedoki said knotting his brows to signify his doubt. "We could make a detour to the north, passing through Ilkiremisho area. Masintet tells me that area is now cultivated and crops are thriving. The catch is that farmers are usually unhappy when pastoralists cross through their territory. The last time we passed through the settled area with my siblings, they warned us to stay clear of their crops. When our cattle strayed into one of their farms, they hacked off their tails, and two had serious cuts on their hind legs."

"So, if we can't cross the river when we get there and can't go round it, then what do we do? Can't we wait until the river is safe to cross again?

"Yes, I suppose so," Kedoki said doubtfully. "But that might be a year or more before it would be again safe to cross."

"You mean the river is swollen the whole year round?" Norpisia asked puzzled.

"Not exactly so," explained Kedoki, "You see, one does not go against the rhythm of nature and expect to be successful in his endeavours. When it is time to cross the river to the southern pasturelands, nature creates favorable climatic conditions that lure domestic as well as wild animals to the rich pastures across the river. Forcing them to go against the natural rhythm would immediately result in the deterioration of their health."

"But if we waited for a year," Norpisia said despairingly, "then we could make it the following year, isn't it? Is there a place where we could set up camp until then?"

"Well, yes, there are people we could stay with, near their *inkangitie*. The Ildamat section of the Maa people have always been friendly. There are families such as Enkang Ole Samante, Eno Ololchoki and Eno Olmagiroi, who are very well known to me and who we could stay with. But I want to get home, Norpisia," he said with a tone which made Norpisia realize how important it was for him to get to Nkararo. "I want us to get settled."

"I want us to get settled too and we should do everything we can to try to get there while it is still safe to cross Enkipai river," said Norpisia thoughtfully. "But if it's too late, it doesn't mean we won't get there eventually. It only means a longer wait."

"That's true," Kedoki said unhappily, only acquiescing in order to bring the subject to an end. "I guess it wouldn't be so bad if we did get home later, but I don't want us to wait around here for a whole year." Then his frown tightened, "I also need to tell my mother what happened to my departed brother and sister." This comment brought the subject to an end. They took their soup in companionable silence as they watched the flames dance over the blackened firewood, leaping and cavorting in their short-lived cheerfulness.

The following day, the team decamped and began their journey through a forest of tall trees, across the Mau highlands. They drove their animals along tracks used by elephants and cattle. They clambered through bamboos on the peak of the highest ridge and then went down across a ravine, walking precariously up the steep banks of a river. Masintet and Lembarta walked ahead of the herd, cutting a way through thickets that blocked them. Suddenly, the two men whistled simultaneously, to alert Kedoki and Norpisia. They had found a lot of tree branches gouged out by elephants that left large puddle footprints and piles of droppings on the forest floor.

Despite the imminent danger, they soldiered on through the slippery and treacherous forest. Every now and then, they found fresh droppings and large bamboo branches uprooted and flung about, their foliage half-devoured, a clear indication that the elephants were not very far. The forest cover was so dense that only pinpoints of sunlight penetrated the canopy to dapple the forest floor.

After treading along for five days in the most difficult climatic conditions, the forest thinned out. Suddenly, sunshine reached them from a blue sky above, warming their shoulders. Emerging from the forest, their spirits were immediately lifted. They gazed speechlessly at the unexpected view before them.

There were the slopes of the Mao-osupuko that Masintet had spoken about. They were expansive lands that were once part of the dense but now decimated Mau forest. It was a mass of patches of grey ashes, blackened tree stumps and lush green shambas that were congested with healthy leafy plants that shone in the sunshine.

Across the valley, they could see the higher cliffs creased by gorges and stubbled by rocks. Traversing the huge man-made plain, like a dying serpent, was river Olorrondo that meandered through naked treeless banks. The river twitched incessantly and gurgled as it meandered around boulders on its way down to join the Enkipai river at Olpurkel lowlands.

Kedoki, Masintet, Lembarta and Norpisia climbed onto a crest and stood in awestruck silence as they looked down on thousands of acres of devastated forest stretching to unimaginable limits. Corrugated iron-sheet roofs that shimmered in the bright sunshine dotted an area that was dominated by bamboo-fenced shambas, now green with waist-high maize plants, purple and white-flowered potato plants and patches of maturing yellow-green millet. On the opposite side were cleared lands stretching for miles and vanishing into the horizon, a deep green immensity of tea plantations on one side and a tawny undulation of ridges of ripening wheat and barley on the other. Randomly, smoke billowed from charcoal mounds that were scattered everywhere while sacks of the black stuff that was in high demand in towns were stacked on paths and roadside. On the few trees that were in sight, vultures perched, staring unblinkingly at nothing in particular, hoping to locate the carcasses of the latest victims of the humans and animals conflict.

"What a pity!" exclaimed Kedoki angrily. "I haven't seen such a thing all my life."

"You have seen nothing yet," said Masintet eagerly. "You should go down to Enoosupukia, Sasimuani or Ilturot-orook. You will then appreciate the extent of the destruction."

"From where I stand," said Lembarta, with a youthful enthusiasm, "I can see as far as Shapa-Iltarakua in that direction and as far as Oloshepani in the other."

"Do you now believe what I was telling you?" Norpisia asked, facing Kedoki triumphantly. "My dreams were a premonition of this scenario and I was told to join wild animals that are fighting humans to stop and reverse this destruction."

"Dreams can at times be misleading," Kedoki said to down-play the significance of Norpisia's dreams. "If you were to join the animals in a mission to fight your fellow human beings you might be the first to be trampled to dust by the agitated elephants or get gored by the angry buffalo."

"If I get trampled to dust or shredded into smithereens while fighting for their right to life so be it," said an agitated Norpisia, her eyes shining with excitement.

"Don't say that, my dear wife," Kedoki said lightheartedly. "Don't you know you are still carrying my sons and daughters in your marrow?"

As they were conversing animatedly, they were suddenly accosted by a large group of men, young and old, who emerged from the bushes behind them, heavily armed with assorted weapons: spears, bows, arrows, axes and pangas. It was Lembarta who saw them first and alerted the rest. They quickly got hold of their own weapons and made themselves ready for any eventuality. They, however, relaxed when they found out that the men were not aggressive. They were pursuing a herd of elephants which had caused massive destruction the previous night and had killed a man. Kedoki explained that they had come across fresh spoors in the forest but did not come face to face with the elephants. Norpisia felt great empathy with the elephants. She nearly told them that they were the aggressors. Nonetheless, the men hurriedly disappeared into the forest, leaving behind an exhausted old man who could not keep their pace. He sat with them chatting about life in their new settlement.

He explained that, apart from the destruction of crops by elephants, baboons that stole their maize, wild-pigs that dug out their potatoes, zebras that fed on their wheat and barley plantations and leopards and hyenas that dragged out their sheep and goats from their pens, life in their new settlement was comfortable. He conceded that although the animals had killed a number of the settlers over the years, they themselves had killed many animals whose meat they feasted on.

"For a long time we have not been slaughtering our animals," he explained contentedly. "We have had a constant supply of meat from hippopotamuses, elephants, buffaloes and elands."

"Did you say the animals have been killing settlers?" Norpisia asked cheekily, a mischievous triumph evident in her voice. "And how often do they do this?"

"Oh yes!" the old man said sadly. "Although we have killed many animals, they too have killed many people. In fact, I would say this is a war over which no side can claim victory."

"Serves you right, you arrogant lot!" Norpisia whispered under her breath, while seething with ire. *"Meirriki intae Enkai neilep!"* she uttered the curse words to herself which meant, she hoped God would lock man and beast in a fierce endless battle. How daring and arrogant have humans become, she thought angrily, to invade the forest, destroy the animal habitat, strip the river banks of the vital undergrowth, and still turn around and accuse the animals of invading their farms! What cheek!

103

The old man looked at Norpisia with sympathetic eyes. What a pity, he thought resignedly, that such a young woman would waste her life wandering in the wilderness following worthless animals that hardly gave any milk and often died in large numbers during droughts. He turned and looked at the three hungry-looking men with her, and thought what a paradox it was that with thousands of cattle, sheep and goats, they should still get hungry! He was like them years back, he reminisced to himself, before he saw the light and took the opportunity when it offered itself, sold the two hundred bony heads of cattle that he owned and acquired a piece of land in the forest. He was now in Canaan, a land where milk and honey flowed freely! He now owned five cows which gave him more milk than the thousand cows gave to their three owners who stood there before him looking hungry and miserable.

He sought leave from them, and when he returned, he brought a basket full of green maize cobs. They lit a fire, roasted the maize and ate with ravenous appetite.

"Would you like to join us, young lady," the old man jokingly addressed Norpisia, "let's share so that you can join us battle the wild animals that cannot allow us to eat our green maize peacefully?"

"Never!" retorted Norpisia emphatically to the consternation of the old man. "If I were to join the fray, I would join the wild animals and fight you for having encroached their natural habitat!"

"You do not need to join them," said the old man

in a fit of pique, having been embarrassed by Norpisia's comment. "The animals have requited our battle with a relentless fierce war that has made many people surrender."

That evening, they decided to set up their camp for the night on top of the ridge overlooking the vast cleared lands that used to be a dense forest. While Masintet and Lembarta cut thorn branches to construct the cattle enclosure, Kedoki joined Norpisia and helped her to off-load the donkeys and unpack their personal effects. Although men did not build houses, Kedoki's love for Norpisia had made him breach some cultural norms, a situation that he knew would be frowned upon by other men if they came to know about it. The six months that he stayed with her while recuperating had drawn them even closer. They had developed a good working rapport that needed little decision making. They both put up the *olngoborr*, anchoring poles into the ground to support the roof that was made of several hides linked and made to overlap, one on top of the other. The oblong, dome-like structure, had an opening at the top to let out smoke, if they needed to make a fire inside, though they seldom did. There was an extra flap sewn on the inside with which to close the smoke opening, if they so wished.

Once the *olngoborr* was up, Kedoki went out to gather firewood while Norpisia lit the fire and began to prepare their evening meal. By the time he returned, Norpisia had a pot humming on one side of the fire-stones, as two hindquarters of mutton boiled. A large chunk of lamb-chops spitted over the flames, with its outer fat layer sizzling.

"Whatever you are cooking smells good," he said cheerfully.

"I am boiling two hindquarters of mutton," she said equally cheerful. "But that is mostly for tomorrow day time. Cold boiled mutton is delicious and soft. For tonight, we shall eat roast *ilaras.*"

The last rays of the sun gleamed through the branches of the trees that surrounded their campsite, as the sun dropped over the edge of the high ground to the west. The setting sun sent up giant red rays that streaked across the sky like the light silky thread which spiders leave on grass and between bushes. Norpisia watched the luminous display for a while. The strange light in the sky worried her. At Olomuruti where she grew up, the red sunset signified danger. She recalled that evening when bandits struck her father's homestead. The setting sun thus had sent up giant red rays, like the one she was watching. The sight was unnerving and she wished she could discern its meaning.

"Does the red glow around the setting sun mean anything in your village?" Norpisia asked Kedoki trying to hide her fear. "In my village it means danger."

"It doesn't mean anything," he answered nonchalantly, hesitant to tell her the belief of his people that when the setting sun glowed with red rays, it was often considered a warning for looming danger.

His reassurance did little to allay her fears. How she

wished her grandmother was with her. She always had an answer for every strange situation. She felt anxious and stressed.

Late at night as she lay awake, she still felt uncomfortable, although she wasn't sure of the reason. It was nothing specific, just a strange edgy feeling. During the afternoon as they roasted the green maize that was given to them by the old man, they had watched rain clouds gathering over the Mau escarpment to the west, seen flashes of sheets of lighting and heard distant rumbling of thunder. Soon after, the clouds cleared and the sky became deep blue with the sun shining brightly. Just then, she heard a sudden deep rolling roar of thunder in the distant. She shot up and sat upright, terrified by the loud booming sound that reverberated and re-echoed in the valleys. In the ensuring confusion in her mind, she heard the voice of her grandmother telling her to quickly get up, and awaken her husband and the other men and immediately flee the area as something terrible was about to happen. Was she dreaming? she wondered, or was her grandmother talking to her through clairvoyance? There was no time to think of that as a bright flash of lightning was almost instantly followed by another loud rumbling boom that shook the ground. She screamed as a deluge poured furiously from heaven followed by the bellowing and bleating of a confused herd.

CHAPTER 10

Norpisia made a bolt for the entrance of the *olngoborr* but before she entered, she immediately retreated when suddenly a burst of lightning flashed through the forest, filling the valley below with an instant dazzling brilliance. She was terror-stricken when a soaring boom tore through the air.

Terrified, she screamed, calling out Kedoki's name in a bloodcurdling shout that echoed in the valley. Kedoki did not respond and she groped her way through the trees confused. The donkeys that always stayed near the *olngoborr*, neighed fearfully, prancing in erratic circles. They sprang out of the animal enclosure and took off into the bushes as though something dangerous was chasing them. The dogs followed, whimpering fearfully.

It began to rain. The wind and the pouring rain washed over her in sheets, almost knocking her down. The rain became heavier and soon, it was raining so hard that she felt as though she was standing under a waterfall. Then, she heard the confused voices of Kedoki, Masintet and Lembarta, hoarsely shouting as they tried desperately to keep the herd within the kraal. Within no time, she heard the cattle break out of the enclosure. They ran headlong tearing through the bushes as they disappeared into the dark night, with the three men in hot pursuit.

Norpisia stood in the rain crying, not knowing what to do. It was dark and the rain complicated everything. Another bolt of lightning enabled her to see Kedoki running fast towards her. He gripped her hand forcefully and dragged her in the direction the animals had gone. In the confusion, she got bruised as she banged and bumped against trees and broken twigs. Although she couldn't see anything in the pitch darkness and the pouring rain, she sensed that they were headed toward the slope leading to the ridge higher up on the escarpment.

They staggered and fell when another burst of lightning flashed and a loud roar of thunder shook the ground violently. They skidded over the slippery ground and darted fast, past a tree that had been struck by lightning and was burning. Before the fire died out, they saw some trees leaning precariously. Then another rumble struck and the trees began to fall.

Although Kedoki still held Norpisia's hand tightly, his grip loosened and she fell. He helped her to stand and urged her to walk on. She could hear his laboured breathing as he panted with exhaustion. The two soldiered on through the wet bushes.

Soon, the rains began to ease up. The trees gave way to thick bushes followed by light bushes and then tall grass. The slope levelled out as the ridge opened out before them in darkness softened slightly by clouds lit by a hidden moon. They stood side by side trying to find their way in the darkness. They felt lucky to have escaped alive.

Just as they thought it was all over a crackling bolt of lightning flashed across the glowing clouds, and descended upon a cluster of tall cedar trees. They leapt into fierce flames, illuminating the valley below.

In the morning, the sun shone radiantly over the landscape. Norpisia and Kedoki stood in bewilderment as their minds slowly came to terms with the desolation that surrounded them. It was as if nature was on a furious revenge mission. Norpisia thought that nature was showing her that she was capable of hitting back, even if she did not join the animals in their war against human beings, as her grandmother had urged her, in her dreams.

When the mist that had hung over the area of devastation had cleared, the green farmlands that they had seen the previous day were no more. Even the shimmering corrugated rooftops that dotted the area were not visible. Either they had been swept away by the raging floods or they were submerged, as the entire valley was now a heaving, swirling stretch of water that moved round in strong circular movements. The Olorrondo river that only yesterday meandered lazily down its outstripped riverbanks, was now vibrant, alive and kicking as it zealously transported down the valley, volumes of water that carried with it uprooted giant cedar trees, great quantities of soil, dead animals and dead bodies of those caught in the storm. A mudslide had ripped off an entire hillside and piled a jumble of boulders and fallen trees halfway across a deep gully, leaving a raw scar of reddish exposed soil. Norpisia stared fixedly at the spot as if spellbound by the scene.

"We were down there," she said sadly. "We would have died had we not managed to get away from those trees before the lightning struck them."

If he had not witnessed most of those events, Kedoki would not have believed them. Even hard to believe, but truthful, were the authentic descriptions of events that were chronologically recounted by Masintet and Lembarta. The two gallant brothers returned to narrate their heroic deeds, having miraculously survived the raging storm. Masintet gave an incredible account of how he and his brother swiftly and blindly followed the fleeing herd. To their utter consternation, Masintet and Lembarta found out later that the animals instinctively knew that there was a looming disaster and therefore they all headed for higher and safer ground on the plateau. When they got there, they found many wild animals had preceded them.

All species of animals had converged there. An agitated herd of elephants stood uneasily on one side, occasionally trumpeting noisily. Buffaloes, zebras, wildebeest and all kinds of gazelles and antelopes mingled with their cattle, sheep and goats, and quietly stood in the rain. Lions, leopards and hyenas hid in thickets, occasionally growling to assert their presence. However, none was aggressive to the other and none was fearful. The plateau was like the legendary Noah's ark. Only human beings were resented by the animals and Masintet and Lembarta spent the night on top of tall trees.

The following morning, when the waters subsided, the wild animals dispersed. The two men climbed down the trees and drove their cattle, sheep and goats, looking for Kedoki and Norpisia, whose fate they did not know. When they counted the animals, they found that they had lost fifteen heads of cattle, forty sheep, ten goats, one donkey and two dogs.

Kedoki and Norpisia could not believe their eyes when they saw Masintet and Lembarta driving back the animals. Kedoki declared emotionally that the two brothers were angels sent by Enkai-Narok, to protect them and their animals. He gave each one of them ten heifers as a token of appreciation for their heroic deeds.

They quickly retraced their steps back to their campsite where they collected their remaining personal effects before driving the animals to the top of the ridge where they remained for a while awaiting the waters to recede.

Kedoki and Masintet discussed the probable cause of the torrential onslaught. Masintet who was a traditional weatherman attributed the cause of the storm to the anger of *Enkai-Nanyokie*, whom he argued was particularly enraged by those who invaded and desecrated Medungi forest, a sacred shrine. Although no blood flowed from the trees, as legend had made people to believe, Masintet thought the death and destruction that they had witnessed following the torrents were enough to show the world the extent of *Enkai-Nanyokie's* fury.

Lembarta, who was a university graduate, reasoned differently. He thought the cause of the torrential pour was climate change occasioned by the destruction of the forests. He said it all began when cold winds blew from Oldonyo-keri mountain in the east, and with atmospheric depressions over the lands whose forest cover had been destroyed, warm moisture-laden air swirled upward and condensed into huge billowing clouds. He explained that when the warm air collided with the cold air from the mountain, the resulting combination brought about the turbulence that created the type of thunderstorm witnessed that night. Kedoki did not dispute any of the two explanations.

Masintet added that before they embarked on their journey to the wilderness to look for Kedoki, they used to see a certain woman who frequented market centres all over Osupuko, telling people who cared to listen to her, to stop destroying forests. Now, with the benefit of hindsight, he thought she must have been a prophetess because what she said then, came to pass. The consequence of wanton destruction of the forest, was there for all to see.

What Lembarta said next, nearly scared them out of their wits. He reckoned that the invasion of the forest and the destruction of its cover were not the only causes of climate change that brought about the freakish rain.

Scientific studies, he said, had revealed that cattle were the worst destroyers of the environment. Could you repeat that? They demanded. According to the report, the grass that the cattle fed on, produced in their guts a gas called methane, which when emitted into the atmosphere through belching and farting, destroyed the environment. The cattle dung, he explained, contained another pollutant, a gas called ammonia. The two gases, he concluded, were said to produce substances that would pollute rivers and accelerate global warming.

The talk was depressing and the trio did not hide their displeasure. Norpisia thought Lembarta's explanation was just a load of crap. Probably, a ploy designed by those who despised pastoralists and intended to bring their nomadic way of life to an abrupt end. But it was Masintet who disabused his brother of what he thought was illogical reasoning. He took him to task about all the ruminants that fed on grass that included wildebeests, buffaloes, gazelles and antelopes, elephants and hippopotamuses. Did they also emit the gases he mentioned or was it a preserve of their cattle alone?

When he could not answer them satisfactorily, they dismissed him as a purveyor of distortions meant to rob them of their means of livelihood.

They did not remain on the plateau for long. When the waters receded and the rivers and streams became fordable, they resumed their journey. The rains that followed the thunderstorm were substantial

114

and they made the green pastures lush and rich. The people who had vacated the Mau forest after the deluge had camped on the western slopes of the escarpment.

Passing through the tsetse fly and tick-infested plains, several heads of cattle died of either rinderpest, east coast fever, or anthrax. Norpisia's herbs came in handy to treat the animals, but at times the sick ones were so many that the herbs ran out before treating all of them.

Seven months later, they stood happily staring at Enkipai river. They were delighted that they were at last going to cross it before it flooded. There was, however, one curiosity: the wild animals that usually crossed the river energetically during that time of the year didn't seem to be very enthusiastic to do so. And the men wondered why.

CHAPTER 11

Two days before they reached Enkipai river, the herdsmen drove their animals across a ravine-creased plain speckled by numerous twisted thorn-trees, wind-bent acacias and the evergreen euphorbia trees. It grew exceedingly hot and the sky was filled by fluffy multi-coloured clouds, a sure sign of blazing days ahead. The abundant game that they expected to find in readiness for their annual crossing to the southern pasturelands were largely absent. As the country grew more and more open, dwarf-whistling thorn bushes appeared. In the distance, they could see herds of gazelles grazing listlessly in the hot sun. And then they saw a pride of lions sloping off into a bushy gully, before climbing onto a cluster of rocks where they stretched themselves lazily.

As they steered their animals away from the ferocious predators, Norpisia saw a cluster of green bushes where a depression was surrounded by tall trees. She thought there could be either a stream or a watering hole down there. Seeing that they had little drinking water left, she took a calabash and went down to fetch clean water. The path zigzagged so sharply downward that she quickly dropped below the heights where soft mist kept the bushes green and growing. When she got to the water point, she found it had dried up. Dry bones scattered in the surrounding area, indicating that predators had been way-laying their prey as they came down in search of water. The sight got her scared, and she feared that a pack of hungry wild dogs or hyenas could easily attack her. She quickly turned back and walked uphill to where the animals were gathered.

There was no respite from the hot sun in the afternoon as Kedoki had expected, so, when he saw Norpisia walking from the watering hole holding an empty calabash, he realized that the area was drier than he had expected. It appeared as though they were now in the full eye of the sun and the baked earth gave back its blast like firestone. The herd was restless and thirsty.

Later in the afternoon, they drove their livestock across the plain as they looked for a safe place to construct a camp. Bare crooked bushes of *Oleleshua* rose eight to ten feet from the ground and looked whitish grey in the harsh light emanating from the hot sun. Norpisia marched on behind the cattle. The terrain was bad: rough with awkward stones or hot and heavy with loose sand. That gritty sand was the worst of all surfaces to walk over, for every step meant an effort and a drain on her calf muscles.

The whole afternoon took on a timeless, monotonous character. Plodding onwards, Norpisia lost her earlier resentment directed at the supposedly uncaring *Enkai-Nanyokie*. Her sense of horror had gone too and she no longer feared that a hyena or wild dog would attack her.

She thought of nothing but the effort needed to keep going.

At last, the plain began to open out, sloping downward in an arc of sand toward the edge of a dry watercourse. Here, there were thick trees, rising high above the bushes. The huge contorted barrel of a baobab tree held up its meager crest of branches, and a thick curtain of fleshy creepers hung across a high, matted wall of thorn trees. Trees and bushes grew on the banks of the wide sand river and on a dry empty bed that had rugged lines formed by the water during the wet weather seasons.

The river bed had smooth fine sand. Examining the sand, Kedoki saw a spot where a bushbuck had crossed the river, and the pug marks of a hyena. Later, Lembarta, who had gone ahead of the cattle spotted footprints. On examining them closely he found that the whole surface had small, clover-hoofed prints of goats' hoofs. Among those hoofprints were the larger marks of cattle and donkeys. There were also long oblong marks in the sand, the imprints of old tyre sandals. In between, there were tiny, twisting and turning prints, being small clear toe marks of running children. It was obvious that a nomadic family with their flock of goats, a few heads of cattle, and their beasts of burden had passed by.

It was when Lembarta returned to tell his story, that they noticed Norpisia was not feeling well. The heat and exhaustion had taken its toll on her.

When they eventually found the family, Kedoki

exchanged polite talk with the patriarch, a lean, wrinkled old man with cropped grey hair. He allowed them to construct their cattle enclosure next to his own while his wife, a tall slender woman draped in colourful *lesos*, and multi-coloured beads, invited Norpisia into her *Olngoborr*. She handed Norpisia a mugful of milk. After the drink and a few remarks about the need for rain, the woman left Norpisia to rest while she went out to give Lembarta and Masintet their share of the milk. Kedoki and the old man had already served themselves.

Norpisia was about to drowse in the heavy air inside the *Olngoborr* when a small big-eyed girl, in a long frock accompanied by her smaller brother peeped and giggled at her. When she called the little children they ran out still giggling. Thereafter, it was all quiet except the distant sound of lowing cows and the faint light click of crickets. She had nearly dropped asleep when the voices of Kedoki and the old man broke in upon her drowsiness.

"The situation is completely hopeless," the old man was saying. "If the rains fail to fall in the next two months, none of us shall have a single cow to his name."

"It is that bad, eh?" Kedoki said sounding desperate. "What is the best thing to do?"

"No man can give sound advice to another at the moment," the old man said in a sorrowful voice. "Many herdsmen are travelling from the direction you are heading to, and they say not a single blade of grass is still standing in that area. Tens of thousand of cattle have already died. I have already lost a hundred heads of cattle myself."

"What do the people attribute this prolonged drought to?" asked Kedoki.

"Oh, there are as many theories, as the people who tell them," answered the old man dismissively. "None of them seem convincing to me. Some people say the drought has come about because the forests have been invaded, trees cut down, the undergrowth cleared and water catchments destroyed. Others say it is as a result of changed river courses, for dams and for irrigation."

"There are others who say the drought is caused by a certain gas that our cattle produce in their guts," volunteered Kedoki, "which they say pollutes the atmosphere and destroys the environment when emitted into the air!"

"What arrant nonsense!" charged the old man angrily. "Those who say that are nitwits. Have they first checked and found out what kind of gas is produced in their own stomachs and how harmful it could be to the atmosphere? How I wish such people would shut up. This is the worst insult against our cattle and against us pastoralists!"

"They say they have studied that at the university," commented Kedoki.

"Go tell that to the birds!" said the agitated old man. "There is no better school to study about cattle, sheep and goats than at the pastures where we spend our entire lifetime following them and rearing them."

"Did you say rich people have diverted rivers and

that they are now using the water for irrigation?" asked Kedoki, the bitter truth just beginning to dawn on him. "Do they allow other people's livestock to drink from their dams?"

"One of them who I know says the water is not sufficient to irrigate his ten thousand acres of land," said the old man. "Moreover, he has just acquired another ten thousand acres of forest land that he is now clearing. If you want to water your animals from his dam, you will be required to work on his farm for two days in order to have your animals take water for one day."

"With that kind of exploitation," a bitter Kedoki commented, "do we need to ask why *Enkai-Nanyokie* is angry with us?"

Norpisia listened to the conversation with growing exasperation. How could anybody in his right mind divert a whole river for his own selfish interests? How could he do that at the expense of the poor herders who had lost most of their livestock on account of the severe drought? How could he make them work on his farm for two days in exchange of water for their animals? She felt distraught and extremely disheartened.

While Lembarta and his brother, Masintet, kept vigil at the cattle enclosure that night, Norpisia and Kedoki spent their night by the family's shelter.

They left early the following morning, having loaded their donkeys in the pre-dawn darkness and chill. They drove the herd to the direction of Enkipai river, in the first grey light.

The sun peeked above the horizon and a few minutes later, the flowing column of cattle, sheep and goats came into sight in the growing daylight, as they rippled smoothly through the dry dusty plain.

For some strange reasons, Norpisia revelled in the sense of freedom which corresponded to the feel of the expansive stretch of the rolling land around them. The herd had to be driven slowly as most of the cattle were weak due to insufficient grass and water in the drought stricken pasturelands. Norpisia walked leisurely behind the herd, whistling and shouting at a sheep here and a goat there, when they started to break away.

The herd began to tire in the afternoon, the weaker ones falling back. Kedoki who was ahead of the cattle, turned them off the track to the south, where a small tributary of the Enkipai river stretched along the base of a hill. The trickle of water that flowed down formed into a small pool where the livestock drank to their fill. Thereafter, they ascended the hill and began grazing as Lembarta and Masintet watched over them.

Norpisia knew from Kedoki's earlier descriptions that they were getting closer to the Enkipai river. She moved to join him ahead of the cattle while Lembarta took her place at the rear. After walking for several hours, there was still no sign of the great river. But later, the vegetation began to change and it became greener. Below them, between steep riverbanks lay the wide gigantic riverbed. Stretching on each side of the riverbank for about a hundred feet, and flowing down

122

the steep course between boulders was a trickle of water that shimmered in the heat. Above it, the clouds rolled ponderously in a procession across an illimitable blue sky.

Although the enormous precipices that formed the two banks of the river looked impossible to cross, each year when the river was flooded, thousands upon thousands of wildebeests, zebras, elands, buffaloes and other animals plunged down into it recklessly, risking their lives and clambered up steep cliffs to reach the southern grasslands.

Over the years, lions, hyenas, wild-dogs and crocodiles, waited at the edge of water to pull out those animals that appeared weak or dazed after being trampled down by the others during the scramble to cross the river.

That year was, however, different. There had been no rain and, therefore, the river was not flooded. The animals trickled down to the river, but on seeing that the water was at its lowest level, they stared confusedly and then turned back. The predators that lay in ambush also stared hungrily, wondering what was happening to their prey.

Norpisia nudged Kedoki, "Do you think it is safe driving our cattle across the river, just yet? Look at the predators across."

"We may have to tarry for a while," Kedoki answered.

They looked for a safe place to construct their cattle enclosure. They remained in the vicinity of the river, warding off lions and hyenas every night, until they thought it was safe for them to cross Enkipai.

When Kedoki, Masintet, Lembarta and Norpisia crossed Enkipai river at last, together with their animals, there was hardly any water on the riverbed. By then, the drought had become so severe, that the whole plain across the river had become a sprawling limitless stretch of brown bare land, with patches of desiccated brush that dotted the hillocks. On the distant hills, there appeared an occasional tree, beyond which lay a desolate wasteland.

There was neither grass nor water anywhere and the animals became emaciated. Soon, they began to die one after the other. At first, when a cow died, Kedoki felt so bad that he could hardly eat or sleep at night. Even as the drought took its toll of his livestock, lions and hyenas became a menace and pounced on the weakened animals every now and then. Fearing that soon he was going to be without any livestock, effectively becoming an *Oltorroboni*, his days and nights became a nightmare, so much so that whenever a cow bellowed or a goat bleated he stumbled wearily about and compulsively counted the cattle and sheep over and over, hoping that he had not lost another animal.

One morning, he woke up to find that, out of the three hundred heads of cattle that had survived the harsh drought, he had lost two hundred of them in one night, leaving him with less than a hundred.

On that day, they decided to move near the wealthy farmer's farm, and work for him under whatever conditions he demanded, as long as he allowed them to water their animals and save themselves from total annihilation.

CHAPTER 12

Kedoki woke Norpisia very early in the morning. Darkness was just beginning to fade away and the stars still shone, rather faintly, in the sky.

The previous night, the men had debated amongst themselves about which of the two largest farms in the area they could approach first, for the purpose of obtaining casual employment in exchange of temporary rights to water. Would they start with Olmakarr farm or Olkarsiss farm? They had learnt from those who had worked in each of the farms that they had different working conditions. For instance, they learnt that at Olkarsiss farm, would-be workers were required to report at the main gate at seven o'clock in the morning and work non-stop until three in the afternoon. Those who had worked in both farms preferred Olkarsiss farm.

Although the owner was said to be harsh, the foreman was an amiable old man who empathized with the suffering pastoralists, and often allowed them to water their animals in advance, even before they had worked on the farm. The owner of Olmakarr farm was said to be sick and on the verge of death. His son, who was three years ahead of Lembarta at the university, was rumoured to be harsh and callous. He treated workers

125

despicably. But, Lembarta thought that being educated, he was approachable. It was finally agreed that Kedoki would try to find work at Olkarsiss farm first and if he failed, Lembarta would try his luck at Olmakarr the following day.

After a bite of *Olpurda*, they set off at a brisk pace, while doves vigorously cooed in the dew-soaked acacia and silvery cobwebs lay on the tawny blades of grass that were standing.

When they eventually entered the vast Olkarsiss farm, the freshness of the air struck her. It was more sharper and clean. A cool fresh scent of lush green vegetation caressed her nostrils pleasantly. She inhaled the luxurious air, filling her lungs with its invigorating freshness. What a contrast between the fresh air in that farm and the dusty and oppressive air that blasted them daily in the windswept plains. Here, every plant was olive green.

They both slowed down and began to walk cautiously, halting often to scan the landscape. From a distance, they saw a river that cut across the farm. It flowed in a ravine clothed in a dense forest. Around it, the farmland rolled away in an undulating plain on which a ripening crop of wheat rippled in the wind. And very far away, still on the vast farm, a luxuriant forest covered the hills.

The path they were following meandered and cut across a field where nappier grass was grown using the overhead irrigation method. Soon, the wet grass soaked Norpisia up to her waist and wrapped itself around her ankles. Norpisia did not mind the wetness. She had endured enough dust and heat at the plains.

They walked swiftly across fields that were flourishing with robust green plants that thrived under irrigation. Ahead of them lay extensive green and golden fields of ripening maize.

"Look at the cobs," Norpisia told Kedoki excitedly. "They remind me of those brought to us by that old man. Do you remember?"

"I do remember very well," answered Kedoki nonchalantly, his mind fully occupied by thoughts about obtaining casual employment and water for his dying animals. "I do sincerely hope we shall be lucky this morning and get work, otherwise we and our remaining animals are doomed."

By the time they got to the home paddock of the Olkarsiss farm, they had passed through fields blooming with all kinds of crops. There was a field of dark green drum-head cabbages that were bursting open, flowering potatoes with their pink and white petals that blossomed in the morning sunshine, green leafy plants of sunflower and many other green healthy crops.

However, what interested Norpisia most were the livestock on Olkarsiss farm. She stopped and stared, spellbound, at a large herd of black and white pedigree cattle that grazed contentedly on a field of tall green grass. Their udders were amazingly large and heavy. On another field, she was fascinated to see, for the first time, long-bearded Angora goats, with long-haired white coats and horns that faced backward and tapered off to a point.

Further on, she saw numerous woolly merino sheep. They dotted a large field.

"One day, God willing," Norpisia said emotionally, "our cattle, sheep and goats shall look like these."

"Tenejo Enkai," Kedoki said agreeing with her, but hastened to qualify his remark. "But only if our riches shall not be at the expense of others."

"That goes without saying," opined Norpisia.

At the gate, Kedoki and Norpisia found a large group of people standing in small groups, waiting to be picked for casual employment that morning. When Kedoki and Norpisia got closer, the throng of people turned and silently stared at them. Norpisia fidgetted distressfully. She felt uneasy. She felt like an *olobel-kik*, the dung-beetle, toiling anxiously to push a ball of cow-dung across a rough surface.

"Why are they staring at us?" Norpisia whispered to Kedoki anxiously. "Why shouldn't everyone mind their own business?"

"Take it easy, my dear lady," Kedoki told her gently and added soothingly, "We are all job seekers. You should not be intimidated by their stares."

"Some of the people standing there don't look like ordinary job seekers," said Norpisia with a fearful concern. "Some of them look like thugs. Some of the young men are ogling at me impudently."

"Ignore them," Kedoki said getting a little exasperated. "Don't allow them to provoke us and in the process

128

distract us from what brought us to Olkarsiss."

They walked on, coming across a group of women who stood by the road, their arms folded across their chests, gossiping as they stared at Norpisia. That made her sharply aware of the thin *lesos* she was wearing. She suddenly felt dizzy as if she was treading in the air. Kedoki quickly took hold of her arm to reassure her. It was then that he realized the damage caused to her mind by the long isolation in the wilderness. She had become xenophobic and was now wary of strangers.

Still holding her hand, Kedoki steered her straight towards the gate. She clung onto him apprehensively. The women grudgingly made way for them.

"What a beautiful woman she is!" said the voice of a young man at the back of the throng of people. "She is certainly very pretty."

Norpisia stiffened and held Kedoki's arm more firmly. Kedoki glared angrily at the direction from which the remarks emanated.

"I want to go back," Norpisia said suddenly with such finality that Kedoki immediately halted. "I don't want to remain here any longer."

Kedoki looked at her tenderly and thought how amazingly beautiful she was when her face was ashen with discomfiture.

They were delighted when they were ultimately picked for the casual labour. They were led together with others to the edge of the forest where they were handed machetes, to begin clearing the bushes and fell trees.

Norpisia thought about the dream in the wilderness where she heard her grandmother tell her to go to the highlands and join wild animals that were fighting human beings. Since then, she had always regarded herself to be on the side of the wild animals. But there she was, standing next to Kedoki her husband, each one of them holding a panga, ready to join others to clear the forest! It was apparent to her that the survival instinct was stronger than one's conscience. The need to secure watering rights for their thirsty livestock and save their lives, superseded the need to conserve the forest and save the wild habitat. To her surprise, she felt no distress as she swung her panga, left right and centre to clear the bushes.

When she was tired, she stopped and looked around. From a knoll near the edge of the clearing, she looked into the forest before her. It was like a peep into Medungi forest dappled with light in various shades of green. Different kinds of trees seemed to stare back at her, as if accusing her of cruelty and duplicity. Before her were the grey green *Ilpironito* trees, the pale green of *Ilkinye*, the bluish olive-green of cedars, and the dark green of *Iloirienito*, all rippling away into the eye of the sun, like monsters frozen at a moment in time.

At the end of the day, Kedoki and Norpisia were handed a permit that entitled them to water their cattle at Olkarsiss dam for the next two days. They were filled with joy and celebrated their achievement.

The celebration was however, short lived. As if to remind Norpisia of her broken vows, lions roared thunderously in the darkness that night, very close to their cattle enclosure. The roaring made the air vibrate and Norpisia cringed fearfully every time it was repeated. It was like a challenge to her, a kind of threat. For a moment, the roar silenced every other sound, the way a bolt of thunder always did. Luckily the lions did not break in, but Norpisia acknowledged that a warning had been sounded.

The following day, the four agreed that Kedoki and Masintet were to drive the herd of cattle to Olkarsiss farm to water the livestock. Norpisia and Lembarta were to go to Olmakarr farm and take up casual employment in a bid to secure another two days of watering rights.

For some strange reasons, that morning, Norpisia's heart was pervaded by happiness hitherto unknown to her. She felt as if that morning's walk with Lembarta to Olmakarr farm was going to be completely different from any other walk she had ever undertaken in her life. When they began their journey, she felt as if she was leaving behind all her worries in that temporary camp. All the strains, all the irritations and all the fears she had had to bear, were forgotten. Hope, optimism and enthusiasm began to take root in her heart. She began to dream positive dreams. She saw herself exiting the gloomy, despondent and hopeless world, and entering into a world where there was no social stratification, such as pastoralists, herders, nomads, sedentary farmers or any other.

She woke up that morning with a new sense of

wonder. She looked at the light shining on a golden dry twig and the spider web on the thorn bush and they all appeared new to her. She heard the cooing of a dove on a tree as though it was singing a new melodious song, she hoped it would never come to an end. It was the kind of song that gave one a glimpse of what happiness was all about.

On their way to Olmakarr farm, Lembarta told Norpisia everything he knew about the farm. He was well versed for he was born and brought up on that farm where his father worked as a herdsman for many years. The old man who took over the farm from the colonial settler, Munroe, at the time of Independence, was called Olmakarr Lemeiseyeki. Although he was old when he took over the farm, he was said to be hard working, charismatic, and had a will to succeed. He wanted to prove to everyone that an indigenous farmer could take over a farm owned by a *mzungu*, inherit his house, his employees, his livestock, his farm machinery and everything else therein, and efficiently manage them. Indeed, he managed the farm successfully to the admiration of many, until his demise twenty years later.

He was succeeded by his son, Olmakarr Lemeisorri, who was now said to be sick. For twenty-eight years, Lemeisorri ran the farm with an iron hand. During that period, he safeguarded his weakness with his infallible twin weapons: ruthlessness that instilled fear into his employees, and his philanthropy. He employed many people and was a devout Christian. He believed that his faith required that he was one with his workers. Although he was said to be a ruthless disciplinarian, his generosity was said to be legendary. He created and perfected the culture of hand-outs. In the process, there arose an ingratiating lot of people who lugubriously begged for charity. Those people were the ones who became parasitic, depending solely on him like ticks. He was, however, not deceived. He knew many did not deserve his help and only came to whine and sponge on him.

Olmakarr Lemeisorri finally let down his guard, and the armour slipped off his hand. He was said to be suffering from a strange disease that took away all his attentiveness leaving him with only a vestige of his consciousness. He had to transfer the management of Olmakarr farm to his son Barnoti.

Lembarta knew the man they were going to see. They grew up on the same farm although they seldom met. Barnoti lived with his family in the ex-settlers house which was now the family residence, while Lembarta lived with his parents at the workers' quarters several kilometers away. Once in a while they met as boys, when they went hunting small game on the farm. When they reached schooling age, Barnoti was sent to boarding schools away from home, while Lembarta joined local schools. They later met at the university. When they graduated, Barnoti went to work on his father's farm while Lembarta searched for employment in every nook and cranny without success.

Since taking over the management of the farm from his father, Barnoti vowed to bring reforms. Assessing what he owned, he was not impressed. He thought there was need for an overhaul.

He moved from station to station supervising the workers. They knew him since his youthful days and did not regard him with awe like they did his father. They instead despised and dismissed him as an ignorant youngster. When they saw him approach, they sluggishly gave way. But he did not care whether they gave way willingly or grudgingly. He did not care what they thought of him. He realised that the workers lacked visionary leadership. His vision had suddenly crystallized: change, and reforms were inevitable.

He embarked on the process of retrenching old and unskilled workers, replacing them with young and skillful ones. He consulted experts and replaced old machinery. He cut out unnecessary work-related expenditure and curtained all luxurious personal expenses.

After six short years, Barnoti had revolutionized Olmakarr farm. Despite some complaints about harshness and condescension, his success story was on everyone's lips.

Although Lembarta's father was among those who were swept away under Barnoti's reforms, Lembarta did not blame him. He had learnt at the university that an idea whose time had come was unstoppable. And so, when his father's time came he had to go.

Barnoti realized that he was not likely to prosper

as long as he was surrounded by people who lived in abject poverty. He had come to learn that wealth was created from among the rich and there was no way others could prosper as long as he monopolized the natural resources that determined their fate. It was then that he decided to construct water troughs outside his farm that would enable all herdsmen to water their livestock freely and without any restrictions.

The other realisation was that there was a high correlation between the rampant environmental degradation, especially the destruction of forests and water catchment areas, which in turn fueled the virulent conflict between people and animals. Of late, elephants, zebras, wildebeests and other animals had invaded their farms in search of foliage and water. In the process, they trampled on and destroyed crops, dams and other infrastructure. They also killed many people.

To remedy the situation, he knew he needed the support of all his neighbours, pastoralists and sedentary farmers. He needed to bring them together to start afforestation programmes, dig dams to provide water to wild animals in their habitat and rehabilitate water catchment areas.

So, when Norpisia and Lembarta arrived at Olmakarr farm, they were surprised to be met by a reformist who immediately gave them free access to water. Not just for a few days, but for as long as they needed it.

CHAPTER 13

The atmosphere was hazy and translucent, with giant sprinklers sending jets of water into the air. Birds sang happily on top of the young leafy twigs, telling all that with water and sunshine, the earth would always be a wonderful place. Norpisia and Lembarta walked swiftly across the farm, their hearts gladdened by the fresh fragrance of the morning. Next to the road, the *Olaimurunyai* blackthorn blossomed, its tiny white petals swaying faintly in the cool morning breeze. Deep green twigs moved back and forth in the wind, while tall *Iloirraga* trees cast their shadows over the vast stretches of water that they could see in the distance. In front of them, lay the largest dam Norpisia had ever seen.

Norpisia stood by the dam. The sight was awe-inspiring. How cruel could life be? Her husband lost nine hundred heads of cattle for lack of water, while a huge dam lay there without a cow in sight!

Her reverie was, however, brought to an abrupt end by the sudden appearance of a tall brown man, wearing only brief shorts. He darted fast toward the dam, lifted himself up into an arc through the air and swiftly plunged into the water. There was a burst of the water, waves and smooth ripples as the swimmer made exaggerated motions into the vast stretch of water.

The man, having swum a reasonable distance, turned around and began to swim back, looking at the two. Norpisia and Lembarta could see the man's brown face as he swam towards them. At once, Lembarta recognized him.

"It is Barnoti, the man we are going to see," Lembarta said excitedly. "How lucky we are to find him here alone!"

"Are you sure he is the one?" asked Norpisia confused by the conflicting images in her mind. She could not imagine the awesome man Lembarta described as owning and running the huge Olmakarr farm, frolicking in water like an uncircumcised boy. Suddenly, he lifted his arm from the water and waved at them with a strange grin of recognition across his face.

"He is waving at us," said Norpisia.

"Yes, he is," Lembarta confirmed smilingly. "I think he has recognised me."

Lembarta and Norpisia caught up with Barnoti soon after he was done swimming and had dressed up. On seeing the pair sauntering towards him, he lifted his head slightly and looked at them. He particularly focused his eyes on Lembarta who he had known for many years but had not seen him ever since his family relocated from Olmakarr farm. As they neared, a smile spread across his face, slowly widening until his brilliantly white teeth gleamed against the dark brown complexion of his face.

"So, it's you, my friend Lembarta!" Barnoti said pleasantly as he proffered his hand. "I didn't at first recognize you. Where have you been all these years?"

"I have been in the wilderness struggling to survive," answered Lembarta sheepishly, reluctant to show open acquaintance to a person he intended to ask for casual employment. "The drought has been too severe nearly wiping out our livestock."

"Hope you people have not slaughtered all the wild animals in the wilderness," said Barnoti lightheartedly.

"Not yet, when our herds are no more, we shall resort to killing them in order to survive." Countered Lembarta honestly.

Barnoti's smile lingered on. Then he seemed to remember the presence of a woman who was a stranger to him, and his smile disappeared with a sudden startling abruptness. Lembarta noted the sudden change and he hastened to introduce Norpisia to him, as the wife of a prominent pastoralist called Kedoki, whose animals had nearly been wiped out by the severe drought.

While the two men were conversing, Norpisia took time to observe quietly the stranger who had the power to determine whether their livestock would have water in the next two days. It was difficult to believe that the youthful man who appeared hardly older than Lembarta, was the owner of this great land. She had learnt from Lembarta that his family's vast lands stretched in all directions for distances that staggered the imagination. Their cattle, sheep and goats were said to be so numerous that the many herdsmen and shepherds who looked after them in different parts of the farm, hardly knew that they were working for the same employer. As he turned to look at her, she noted that he was tall, well built and his eyes were solid, gleaming and black.

"What can I do for you?" Barnoti asked abruptly and in such a business-like tone that Lembarta got alarmed.

"We have come to ask you for a favour," Lembarta stammered incoherently, having been caught unprepared. "We are looking for casual employment to enable us secure watering rights for our animals."

"Ah, only that? How lucky you are," the man said, confounding Lembarta further, "You people are indeed lucky."

"Are you saying, sir, that we are likely to get casual employment?" asked Lembarta with a suggestive smile.

"I will give you more than casual employment," the man said without being clear about what he was alluding to. "You follow me."

They briskly followed Barnoti across his farm. Part of the land was not new to Lembarta. They walked through fields that ran along the large dam where potatoes, tomatoes, cabbages, onions and other vegetables were grown under irrigation. On the other side of the fields, lay many workers' houses. They walked through the workers quarters where men, women and children moved about noisily. A large cloud of dust rose on the other side of the dam, where a herd of cattle and flocks of sheep were being moved about. Norpisia noted that the workers' houses were spread out over an area much larger than a large Manyatta would encompass. And there were more people about than there would be in a large ceremonial Manyatta.

They walked on, crossed a valley and climbed up a hill, onto a flat ground. Lembarta at once knew Barnoti was leading them to his home compound. Soon they were there. Norpisia saw trees that towered into the sky to a dizzying height. Below them were clusters of smaller trees. Between the trees and under their shadows was a large house with a wide veranda. Next to the main house were four or five smaller houses with trees clustered around them with wide sweeps of green shrubs between them. The verandas had climbing vines hanging around them in thick mats.

Then Lembarta and Norpisia saw an old man. He was dressed in a loose dressing gown, his grey hair seemingly unkempt. He leaned heavily on his walking stick as he walked. His face was heavily lined and wrinkled. Lembarta whispered to Norpisia that the old man was Lemeissorri, Barnoti's father, who was said to be sick and dying.

The old man's steely, grey eyes fastened on Norpisia. When he got close to where they were, the old man stopped, leaned on his walking stick and waited. Norpisia quickly walked up to the old man, stopped a few feet from him and bent her head in greetings. He lifted his hand and lightly touched the top of her head.

"*Nakerai,*" he called out in a weak voice.

"*Yeo,*" answered Norpisia showing great reverence for the old man.

"*Supa!*"

"*Epa naleng papaai,*" she answered, making obeisance and then moved away from him.

Lembarta also moved to where the old man stood and proferred his hand which the old man barely touched.

Barnoti introduced Lembarta and Norpisia to the old man and completely out of their wildest expectation, Barnoti told his father that he had decided to assist the unfortunate pastoralists who had nearly lost all their livestock through the severe drought by allocating them part of the farm where they would graze the remnants of their herd until it rained. Their herd would be free to drink from the scattered watering troughs.

Norpisia was simply ecstatic. Lembarta could not believe his ears, having known how harsh and heartless Barnoti had been. He likened him to Saul who, when he saw the flash light on his way to Damascus, changed his hitherto bellicose behaviour to become Paul the man who preached peace.

The news Norpisia and Lembarta carried back to their temporary campsite was indeed joyous. However, when they got back, they found Masintet in a gloomy mood. Kedoki too appeared disheartened and miserable. Something seemed to have gone terribly wrong.

"What unending woes!" Kedoki blurted out dejectedly. "When we thought we had surmounted one problem, another one sticks out like a sore thumb."

"What has happened again, my husband?" Norpisia asked quickly. "Have we lost some more cattle?"

"Not yet, but we shall soon lose all of them," Masintet answered resignedly.

"Today our cattle did not pick a blade of grass," explained Kedoki despairingly. "You see, there were so many herds of cattle waiting on the line to be watered that by the time we got a chance to water our herd, it was already late in the evening. Although they quenched their thirst, the flock did not graze at all. They are therefore very hungry."

"The founder said, *edoorie emodooni nkuta*," said Lembarta jovially, meaning, an old blind sheep that is thirsty, sometimes stumbles upon a pool of rain water.

"What do you mean?" Masintet asked his brother quickly.

"We found the moon feeding!" Norpisia said metaphorically.

Kedoki and Masintet sat up suddenly, stunned by Norpisia's use of the rarely quoted metaphor. They knew that the metaphor meant one had unexpectedly come into contact with generous super human spirits that did something out of the ordinary.

"Please explain," said Masintet impatiently.

"Tell them," Norpisia told Lembarta triumphantly.

"It's good news for all of us and our cattle," Lembarta explained. "We went to Olmakarr farm to ask for casual employment. And what did we get? The owner of Olmakarr gave us a gift that is difficult to imagine. He allowed us to move into his farm, graze and water our animals until it rains."

"Do you mean Barnoti himself, agreed to this arrangement?" asked Masintet doubtfully, having known Barnoti and his heartlessness in the past. "You must have been duped!"

"And what are we expected to give in return?" asked Kedoki suspiciously. "I hope it is not a ploy to take away the animals from us."

"If I didn't know Barnoti very well, I would have thought someone with sinister motives was impersonating him to lure us into a trap," explained Lembarta confidently.

"Moreover," added Norpisia convincingly, "The man took us to his father to whom he explained his intentions."

"My brother Lembarta knows Barnoti as much as I do," Masintet said disconcertingly, "We both grew up with him on the Olmakarr farm. He ruthlessly dealt with elderly workers, including our own parents. Unless it is *Enkai-Narok* who is intervening on our behalf, it is difficult to believe that the arrogant brute could proffer such a kind gesture out of his own volition."

A lively debate ensued about their rights and freedoms while living within the confines of the farm. At the end, they reached a consensus on the matter. They agreed to move into Olmakarr farm the following morning on condition that they reserved the right to move out immediately, if their freedom or cherished cultural dignity were infringed. For, as Kedoki concluded

"It is better to die poor but dignified."

Early the following morning, as they gathered their few belongings and grouped their livestock, ready to move, a strange phenomenon took place. Four young wildebeest calves, one male, three females, appeared from the bush and ran into the herd, seeking lactating cows in order to suckle. The cows kicked and warded them off, while dogs barked at them. Kedoki, Masintet and Lembarta watched with consternation. What did that portend? Was it a message from the spirits' world? They wondered.

But when Norpisia appeared at the scene, she did not look surprised. She told her husband what she had told him before: that she once dreamed of being asked to go to the highlands and join wild animals to fight human beings who were destroying the animals habitat. Maybe, she said, the forces that destroyed the animals' habitat were now finally defeated, and the four young wildebeests were symbolically sent by the gods to accompany their cattle and victoriously match into their liberated habitat.

"No, no, no!" protested Masintet. "That explanation cannot hold water. I think that is merely a figment of Norpisia's imagination!"

"My friend Masintet," Kedoki warned ominously. "Do not dismiss her words thoughtlessly. I have learnt that most of the things she says come to pass. On many occassions, what she portends has serious consequences."

That afternoon found the trio and Norpisia in the expansive Olmakarr farm. True to his word, the indefatigable Barnoti had made all necessary arrangements to receive them and their livestock. Norpisia did not leave behind the four young wildesbeest calves, that she fed cow milk using a bottle-like container called *Esiorog*. They mingled with the domestic animals and moved alongside the cattle.

Salaash, who once lived with Lembarta and Masintet on the farm, was asked by Barnoti to usher in the pastoralists and direct them to the reserved pastures, and the two houses that had been allocated to them. The houses were within the workers' quarters, and immediately behind them was a cattle enclosure where their animals would be herded at the end of day. After seeing all that generosity, Kedoki agreed that truly, Norpisia and Lembarta had found the 'moon feeding'!

At almost sunset, Norpisia and Kedoki contendedly walked across the large workers' camp, toward the house that had been allocated to them. Many workers were arriving from their work stations and they exchanged pleasantries.

As Norpisia lit a fire in front of their house they saw a man carrying a lantern walking across the open space toward them, the lantern casting a yellow glow on the dusty ground. The stranger was carrying a pail in his other hand. The dogs that lay near the fire quickly rose up on seeing him approach and barked fiercely. Kedoki immediately recognized the approaching man. He was Salaash, the man who ushered them into Olmakarr farm.

"Is it you, Salaash?" Kedoki called out happily.

"Yes, is it safe for me to come nearer or will I be mauled by your fierce dogs?"

"It is safe," Norpisia said pleasantly. "Please do come in."

Salaash held up the lantern as he approached the entrance of the house.

"We butchered an ox," Salaash said jovially. "And the boss asked me to bring you some meat."

Norpisia thankfully took the pail from the man's hand. "We can never thank him enough for his immeasurable generosity."

The pail was full of fresh meat. The smell of the blood and meat was rich and heavy. Kedoki thanked Salaash profusely. When Salaash left, Norpisia began to prepare their evening meal and Kedoki went out to check on Lembarta and Masintet at their one-roomed house. Just a day before, he was sinking deep into the quagmire of desperation and despondency. He could not help but belt out a song they used to sing when they were carefree Morans:

Natijinga inkonyek iltiale,	My eyes have become dim,
Aimariri inkoitoi rongeni	As I continuously gaze at the narrow paths.
Nikiimie inkishu ang kireu linka	Through which we'll drive our cattle to the lush green pastures.
Linka naitopiu isuam ang	Lush green pastures that shall revive our cattle.

He looked forward to a peaceful night. He did not expect to hear the howling sounds of the wild dogs, devilish laughter of the hyenas or the humbling roar of the lions. Little did he know that the irrepressible teasing habit of Masintet would not allow him such a luxury.

"The days of maladroit and blundering Lesiote have at long last come to a dead end, my friend," Masintet said hilariously as soon as Kedoki arrived at the fireplace. He laughed and danced about as he slapped Kedoki on the shoulder. "What excuse will you give to her tonight for not showing her what your manhood is made of?"

"Get off my shoulder!" Kedoki shrugged his shoulders feigning anger, while chuckling good-humouredly. "You are such an incorrigible trouble-maker."

"I don't want to waste my time with you," said Masintet teasingly. "Go back to your beloved wife, you good-for-nothing Lesiote!"

"I will show her tonight that I'm not Lesiote," vowed Kedoki as he roared with rich mirthful laughter, "You will soon begin seeing my sons and daughters following one another like *Ilanguda*."

Soon, Masintet and Kedoki were discussing more serious issues. They talked about the need to uphold dignity befitting honourable guests, as long as they remained on the farm.

After supper Kedoki walked under the dim light of the half-moon. Before he entered his new house, he looked up and gazed at the brilliance of the fleet of stars that always teased his mind with their numbers, remoteness and their mystery. However, he thought the greatest mystery was what life held for him and Norpisia as they plunged into the wilderness on the last leg of their journey to Nkararo.

CHAPTER 14

Kedoki and Norpisia had never had it so good. For the first time since they got married, the couple was able to live in their own house as husband and wife. While Kedoki enjoyed the privilege of coming home in the evening to find a hot meal and a warm welcoming house, Norpisia, for the first time since leaving her father's home at Olomuruti, had had the undivided attention of her husband. And she basked in the enthralling love that he constantly showered her. Soon, Masintet's teasing habits came to an abrupt end when it became evident that the happy couple was expecting their first child.

The rich pastures of Olmakarr farm immensely benefited Kedoki's livestock. His personal expertise in animal husbandry, the availability of lush green grass, plenty of clean water and salt licks that were given ad lib, turned the recently emaciated walking skeletons into admirable healthy animals. Even Norpisia's wildebeest calves had grown to full-blown adult animals that grazed alongside the cattle.

Lembarta and Masintet continued to live with Kedoki and Norpisia. They knew nature had favoured them because the ten heifers that Kedoki gave each one of them had survived the severe drought. With the favourable condition on Olmakarr farm, the two brothers looked forward to nurturing their budding herds with the hope that one day, they would too, drive a large herd of cattle and be received back in their village at Eorr-Narasha as heroes.

While Barnoti appeared to have become a coveted environmental conservationist, his neighbours, including his immediate neighbour, the owner of Olkarsiss farm, continued to destroy the forests and water catchment areas. The owner of Olkarsiss farm in particular, was at that time on an expansion mission. He was in the process of clearing ten thousand acres of forest land to give way to a tea plantation. When Barnoti persuaded him to desist from destroying the forest, he argued that tea bushes were environmentally friendly and that contrary to what Barnoti and others thought, tea plantations were part of environmental conservation measures. He laughed contemptuously at Barnoti's concern that the trees he was felling helped to bring rain and conserve the environment. The owner of Olkarsiss farm argued that rain came from the blue-bellied god called *Empus-oshoke*. Armed with that argument, the expansionist of Olkarsiss cleared the forest with such vindictiveness that one would have thought he harboured a grudge against the trees. Day and night bulldozers boomed and roared in the forest. Poor pastoralists, who sought watering rights at the farm, had to work for long hours, clearing, gathering and burning the undergrowth.

For many weeks that followed, bulldozers felled trees, and heaped them, while workers moved from heap to heap, torching them. Every night, from across the boundary fence, Kedoki and Norpisia watched the distant fires at Olkarsiss and other adjoining farms, as they crept and writhed like giant monsters, consuming everything on their paths. By day, dark clouds of smoke billowed up from the hills and valleys with red amber flames sticking out from them, like giant fierce tongues. Dust rose from the bare fields and danced in whirlwinds that formed and disappeared with the waywardness of mirages. Dusty tree branches, withered grass, and forest life were all instantly sucked up and consumed. Even the deep and wide river that in the past rumbled across Olkarsiss farm was now exposed to the rays of the sun.

One night, the fire got out of control and quickly spread into other farms in the vicinity. It spread into part of Olmakarr farm where the grass was already brown and withering. At night, Norpisia and Kedoki could see the fires winking like the eyes of *Inkipuldianyi* in the dark. Norpisia could imagine ants, beetles, crickets, cicadas, birds, chicks, tortoises, snakes, rodents, young ones of gazelles, wildebeests, and many, others roasting in the fire and perishing, all because of man's insatiable greed. She felt sad and angry. Kedoki and Norpisia knew that as the fire spread, devastating Barnoti's Olmakarr pastures, thousands of his flock would starve.

On one of the days, several months after the fire spread over many grass fields and consumed all pastures,

Kedoki accompanied Lembarta and Masintet in search of patches of grass that had survived the scorch. The felling of trees, the clearance of the undergrowth and the general destruction of the environment had intensified the drought in the area. Even at Olmakarr farm where the owner had laid out great irrigation plans, the land was now succumbing to environmental degradation. There was no longer enough water in the large dams to irrigate the fodder fields. As a result, nappier grass, *alfalfa,* as well as maize plants were wilting in the fields. Barnoti's zero-grazed pedigree animals would soon die of starvation.

Kedoki feared that before Barnoti's livestock died of starvation, his would have died well in advance, for by then, he knew Barnoti would have understandably asked him to move his animals out of Olmakarr farm.

Kedoki was silent most of the day. He only replied absent-mindedly to questions from Lembarta and Masintet. He walked with them silently as they drove their livestock to the watering point at the dam's fast receding shore-line and later in the afternoon as they moved the animals from paddock to paddock in search of grass.

In the evening, they drove their animals back into the enclosure and went into Kedoki's house where Norpisia had prepared their evening meal. They sat on stools around the fire and ate their food in companionable silence. At sunset, when the shadows gathered, Lembarta and Masintet left for their house. As soon as they were out of earshot, Norpisia stirred the fire and then looked sternly into Kedoki's face.

"There is no need for you to keep silent day and night," she told him candidly. "It is no secret that the fires we have been seeing in the last few days and the hardening drought we are witnessing are sending us a clear message. It is time for us to move out of Olmakarr farm before we are eventually thrown out."

Ever since Kedoki married Norpisia, there was nothing that he longed for than taking her to his village at Nkararo and showing her off as his beloved wife. When he left Olomuruti with her, he had envisioned a day when he would triumphantly arrive back at Nkararo village driving his over one thousand heads of cattle, hundreds of sheep and goats, and being met by a singing and dancing crowd. Although he lost a brother and a sister to the cruel hands of bandits, he knew the villagers would understand they died in the course of defending what Enkai-Narok had given them at the beginning of time. They would probably appreciate his bravery and fearlessness in having gallantly driven his large herd through the wilderness.

However, that was not to be. He wondered whether it was worth going back to the village shamefully, driving a depleted herd of less than a hundred cattle. Although he loved Norpisia dearly, she could not be a substitute for the hundreds of cattle that he lost. He wondered whether he should tarry in the wilderness once more, after vacating the Olmakarr farm, with the hope that it would rain soon and that his cattle would once more flourish and multiply. He would then venture back to Nkararo. But would Norpisia and the infant in her womb survive the harsh life in the wilderness?

At the same time, he knew that a man had to do what he felt had to. But whether it was due to her pregnancy or due to the dullness and monotony of living day in day out in a sleepy dusty workers camp, he noted that Norpisia had developed mood swings and complained a lot. Nevertheless, he was careful not to infuriate her. Most of the time, when she complained or when she raised an argument, he did not give an instant reply or raise a counter argument. He gave himself time to reflect upon what she said and then gave her an answer that he thought would mollify her.

He had also noted that she had become obsessed with the need to save wild animals and preserve their habitat. In the wake of those fires, she had nightmares in which she saw frightful images that left her sweating and trembling. He recalled one night when they were sleeping peacefully, she suddenly sat up, threw her blanket off and bolted for the door. He quickly got out of bed and darted after her, grabbing her as she opened the door. He held her tightly as she slowly came back to her senses and realized where she was. She was shaking and the thin *leso* she wore was soaked in perspiration.

She had had another nightmare, she explained. They stood at the doorway looking at the fires blinking away on the ridges across Olkarsiss farm. Hyraxes that seemed angry at the fire, screeched wildly in a full-throated chorus that effectively drowned the nightly croak of frogs at the dam. When she had calmed down, she explained that she had dreamed of big animals, elephants, rhinos, giraffes, buffaloes and wildebeests running around in confusion, their huge bodies burning, making them look like giant moving torches. Then her grandmother appeared in the dream, complaining bitterly that she had not heeded her advice to join animals in the highlands and fight alongside them to reclaim their habitat. Before she woke up, her grandmother was telling her to ask her husband to brand the four wildebeests that were in their herd, with their brand marks and ensure that the wildebeests remained in their herd all the time. That dream had left him wondering what it portended.

Kedoki reminisced on a legend that he was once told when he was young. It said all wild animals once belonged to women. The women were said to have been richer than men who only owned cattle, sheep and goats, while they owned all the wild animals in the world. The legend had it that when the women got pregnant, they craved for certain sweet bluish fruits called *Isanangurrurr*. They went looking for them in the bushes. Each time they plucked some from one bush, they saw more luscious ones in the next bush. They went on plucking the sweet fruits and forgot their animals which went astray and got lost in the wilderness. And that was how, the legend concluded, the women lost their animals and had to live with men in order to share their possessions.

"My silence is not ill-motivated, my dear wife,"

Kedoki said at long last. "There is need for us to move out of Olmakarr farm before we are thrown out."

"What have you decided?" she asked coldly.

"Nothing so far," he answered calmly. "I have all along been thinking of your present condition, wondering how we would manage the harsh conditions in the wilderness if we were to leave Olmakarr farm now."

"I shall manage," she said curtly and added arrogantly, "after all, one is ultimately responsible for his or her own well-being."

"That is true, my wife," he said kindly trying to avoid an argument that he knew she was building up. "I'm solely responsible for your well-being."

"Do you know the reason why the founder said somebody else's cow dries up in the day time?" she asked excitedly, beginning to initiate an argument. "I believe he wisely meant that a thing that belongs to another could be taken away without warning. Similarly, whether we like it or not, we might be asked to vacate Olmakarr farm the moment the owner thinks our cattle are competing for grass with his."

"Leave all these to me," he told her soothingly.

He later came to know the reason for her anxiety and the cause of her arrogance. She was greatly stressed and later became extremely restless as the moment for giving birth approached. It was at midnight that he went out to look for *enkaitoyoni*, the village midwife. When she came, she ascertained that Norpisia was indeed in labour. He left her with the midwife and went to look for Lembarta and Masintet. She was in labour for nearly twenty-four hours, for it was not until the next day midnight that he was informed that she had had a difficult but safe delivery. It was a great relief. He had been anxious and restless the whole day.

When he entered his house, he saw the midwife crouched by the fire. She looked like a grotesque figure with a blanket wrapped around her shoulders, her eyes swollen and red from lack of sleep and the effect of smoke from the fire. She ushered him into the other room where Norpisia was, so that he could see the baby. Norpisia was asleep, looking ashen and exhausted. The baby boy was big, wrinkled and reddish. He was already yawning and sucking his fingers hungrily. Kedoki carefully tucked the blanket around Norpisia and the baby and stealthily backed out of the room.

Later in the day as he looked after the livestock, he thought of the baby's name. He settled on the name Kinyamal, which meant to be born at the time of trouble.

Norpisia took almost two months to recover; the birth of her baby had been difficult. Her recovery would probably have taken much longer had it not been for the anticipated arrival of a much-talked about woman that Lembarta and Masintet once likened to a prophetess. She moved from village to village, trading centre to trading centre talking about the hazards of climate change, which she attributed to the general environmental degradation. Her movement was said to be gathering momentum and more people were listening and following her from one meeting to another. What was exciting people, was that whatever she said invariably came to pass.

It was said she recently visited a village which had not had a drop of rain for close to two years. She told a gathering that their woes were caused by the wanton destruction of forests and water catchment areas. She spoke of erratic climate conditions that would be witnessed in future. But because of the drought that persisted for a long time, people could not believe her when she told them to be prepared for they might be caught up in a sudden downpour. In the dry heat, dust and flies and the winds that blew across the bare ground, it was hard for the villagers to believe that it would ever rain again. Women had even neglected the roofs of their houses that normally required constant attention.

Two days after she left the village, quite unexpected thunderstorms suddenly burst with unrestrained ferocity. The lightning that followed was vicious. Its great crackling tongues blasted any men, animals or trees in its path. Dung plastered as well as grass thatched roofs leaked so badly that many families, for the next few days, lived in a quagmire. That story terrified Norpisia and Kedoki, for it was reminiscent of the destructive storm that caught up with them two years earlier at the edge of the forest.

So, when Norpisia heard that the so-called prophetess was likely to visit the area, she was curiously excited. She wanted to see her and hear her talk. For unknown reasons, she somehow felt connected with her, as if her fate was linked to the prophetess. And she thought the urge that she had had ever since that dreadful nightmare when her grandmother asked her to join wild animals to fight for the preservation of their habitat, would be realized the day she met the prophetess. The excitement she now felt helped to enhance her recovery.

When Norpisia asked Kedoki how the four wildebeests were fairing, he did not at first think the question had anything to do with the anticipated arrival of the prophetess. In fact, the question had him jokingly thinking that she, in line with the legend he had heard, was out to reclaim the animals that women lost. He told her the four beasts had assimilated well into their herd. And when he told her that he had branded them with the marks of his clan as she had requested, she seemed happy.

"It may be a tiny victory," she told him quietly. "But the day you accepted to allow the four wildebeest calves to remain in our herd against the wishes of Lembarta and Masintet, you enabled me, to some extent, to fulfil my grandmother's wish."

"We should have known what we were getting ourselves into," Kedoki told her seriously, "I can foresee hard times coming our way soon. The moment Barnoti comes to know that we brought along worthless beasts to graze upon his pastures, he would definitely throw us out."

"Why do you think so?" she asked nonchalantly. "After all, what are four beasts in the midst of a hundred heads of cattle?"

"It is not a question of numbers," argued Kedoki calmly. "It is simply that the four good-for-nothing beasts are eating grass that four milk producing cows should be eating. Even though I can see your desire to fulfil your grandmother's wish I would rather have one sick cow in my herd rather than a thousand worthless wildebeests milling around me like maggots on a festering wound."

"What a thing to say!" Norpisia said aghast at his words, "It is not the worth of wildebeests we should be looking at when we consider protecting them. We should know that all creatures, from the tiny dung-beetle to the giant elephant are all our cherished heritage bequeathed to us by *Empus-oshoke*, the blue-bellied god."

"When it comes to fighting to retain our heritage," murmured Kedoki in a quiet emphatic tone, "I would certainly join you."

"Then we must join the prophetess," said Norpisia emphatically, "I believe she represents the forces of sanity that are fighting to resuscitate the soul of our drying land."

"We must be on the prophetess' side," Kedoki said seriously as he looked into the distant hills beyond Olkarsiss farm where the last ray of the setting sun touched the red and crimson clouds. "And I can assure you, my beloved wife, we shall win."

CHAPTER 15

Norpisia was among the villagers who burned with curiosity to meet the famous prophetess. For the last one month word had spread like bush fire announcing the anticipated arrival of a woman who had become a heroine to many and an object of hate and derision to others. In the eyes of the pastoralists who had suffered from the severe weather conditions, she was courageous and outspoken. She was said to have fearlessly confronted matters of environmental degradation with the aim of rehabilitating the destroyed water catchment areas.

The sun was rising over the Enkipai plains and spreading its thin ruddy light over the Ereteti trading centre which sprawled at the edge and foot of the Endikirr hill. Approaching the trading centre from the east, Eddah Sein, the prophetess saw first the disorderly stretch of tin-roofed hovels situated within the extreme end of the Olmakarr farm and which housed some of its workers.

Walking through the yet-to-wake-up large centre, Eddah Sein gave thought to her role in that community. Although her admirers called her a prophetess, she did not consider herself to possess any qualities that would make her one. She did not prophesize anything that came to pass as it was widely believed. What she did in the public meetings she hosted, was to explain the known consequences that naturally followed the wanton destruction of forests. She knew what she talked about, for she was highly educated on matters to do with the environment. She was also equally and well versed in the world of art, culture and intellect. Those who knew her well, said she was a woman of high self esteem who mingled freely with the lowly pastoralists and was at home among the foremost in society. It was also said that no one could put her down or mock her. Whoever tried to do so, was at risk for she was known to excite public passion. As a result, she was unassailable. She was always beyond the reach of those who would have liked to put her down.

At six o'clock in the morning, Eddah Sein walked from Ereteti trading centre where she had left her small car, to Olmakarr farm where she was to plant tree seedlings in an area where the forest was recently destroyed. As she walked across the sprawling Ereteti trading centre, she marvelled at the speed at which the unknown town had grown. Ten years earlier when she used the route with her parents on her way to and from school, there was no trading centre to speak about then. At that time the place was famously known as *Duka Moja*, for by then, it boasted of an only shop, a shabby structure built of wood and rustic corrugated iron sheets. It stood beside a narrow deep-rutted road. It was the place where cattle traders stopped overnight to rest their exhausted animals, in order for them to regain strength to face the series of steep escarpments which rose up sharply from the plains to the lofty Mau ranges. The centre had grown into a large haphazardly planned shanty-town. As she walked through the narrow earth road that twisted in and out between tumble-down hovels, she cast her eyes to see the kind of life lived there. At certain places, the road became so narrow like a footpath. She observed that it was in those hovels that the deadly illicit brew called *changaa* was distilled and consumed in large quantities. And it was in those dark alleys that the blinded and the dead victims of the deadly concoction were regularly fetched for onward transmission to hospitals and mortuaries. It was in this same place that a particularly unpleasant brand of cigarette and hard drugs were sold. Soon, she emerged from the slum and walked into the affluent part of the centre. It had neatly spaced stone buildings with plate glass shop fronts and hotels. Bougainvillea, golden shower and morning glory flowers blazed in little gardens. The main street was an avenue of rather spindly jacaranda trees.

She realized as well as anyone else that the rapid growth of the centre was attributed to the wealth that poured in from coffee, vegetables and cereals. They were grown in the lower ridges of the newly acquired forestlands. Pyrethrum, milk, wheat and barley from the rolling uplands and the dense forests on top of the Mau ranges had also accelerated the growth of Ereteti and other mushrooming and swiftly growing towns in the newly settled areas. Within the destroyed forests was the sale of timber and other forest products as well as the sale of trophies obtained from poached wildlife. She thought it was only recently that the inhabitants of Ereteti and other areas in the country had woken up to the realization that nothing that was mismanaged lasted for long. It was now a fact that the wantonly destroyed forests were no more, and the timber industry had been brought to a halt. The elephants, rhinos, cheetahs, leopards and other games had been poached to near extinction.

The Ereteti trading centre now sat ill among the environmentally degraded volcanic hills. The drought-devastated yellowish plains with a few gnarled old trees meant nothing to its inhabitants. The heat and glare reflected from the overtrodden bare ground was unbearable at midday and it sent everyone hurriedly looking for shades. They did not notice that the red dust that blew from the hills was doing so with increasing strength and fury. Ignorantly, they were only too glad that the delayed rain gave them ample time to burn charcoal uninterruptedly. Charcoal burning being the only other business available after the timber industry had collapsed – until they found out that the lengthening spell of dry weather had dried up the only river that was the source of their drinking water.

Perhaps the people did not fully realize that the drying rivers and depleted pastures were mother nature's own way of letting the environment destroyers know that she was finally through with them Eddah

Sein thought. The people would perish if they did not institute immediate remedial measures to resuscitate the degraded environment.

Soon, she left the town and took the road that led her to Olmakarr farm. At a small church on the roadside, she recalled her younger days when she was introduced to christianity and converted into the faith. She remembered her boundless joy and respect for church elders who she thought had ardent love for their flock.

In those days, she had steadfast faith not only in the church, but in the individual elders who ran it. She did not at that time know that the christian foundations upon which her life had been built, were slowly crumbling away beneath the heavy load of greed and corruption, seen in the grabbing of forest land, impunity, duplicity and the destruction of the environment. Ironically, the first to commit those evils were those who preached against them.

When she thought of the owners of Olmakarr and Olkarsiss farms who were known to be staunch christians, she felt sad for them. She wondered how they reconciled their conscience, with their greed demonstrated in their grabbing of thousands of acres of forest land and the diversion and damming of rivers for their own exclusive use, denying all other pastoralists water for their livestock.

At thirty-five years of age, Eddah Sein felt fit and energetic. She looked up towards the hills in whose giant bosoms lay the expansive Olkarsiss farm. She could see tractors tearing through vast acreages of virgin lands which, only recently, were covered by dense forest. The hot wind had not risen and all was still calm and clear in the crisp freshness of early morning. But she noticed the red dust being blown from the bare hills and which settled on each blade of grass and on every leaf. It angered her to think that the greedy expansionist farmers destroyed the forest without giving a hoot as to who was affected by their actions.

So when the people heard that their beloved prophetess had arrived, they turned up in big numbers, each one of them holding a bunch of tree seedlings for planting. They accompanied her to an area adjacent to Olmakarr farm and listened to her attentively as she enumerated the woes that were brought about by the wanton destruction of the forest. She led them in planting the indigenous tree seedlings they had brought. She had chosen an area that was adjacent to Olmakarr farm to symbolize future activities in that area where the forest was destroyed. Wherever she planted trees, she always erected a bill-board with a picture of a green tree, which she said was a symbol of life.

When she addressed them, she emphasized that all people had equal rights to the forest resources. She said no one had the right to cut down trees indiscriminately, and added that certain forests such as Medungi and Naiminie-enkiyo were protected through cultural proclamations and prohibitions made by *Oloiboni* from time to time. She emphasized the fact that forests were the source of rivers, herbal medicine, sacred trees and shrubs that solemnized ceremonies and which held their people together. Simply put, forests were the source of life.

She likened the forest to a cloak that covered and shielded the body. The roots held the soil together and prevented soil erosion while the undergrowth prevented moisture from evaporating. Rivers, she explained, were kept cool by the forest cover and free from pollutants by their interwoven roots that filtered the underground water seepage. Tree leaves absorbed polluted air and other gases in the atmosphere, enabling people to breath fresh air.

When she explained the link between forests, rivers and pastures, the people began to understand the genesis of the drought. They could now see how the wanton felling of trees, the clearing of the undergrowth and the destruction of water catchment areas had all worked together to destroy the environment, resulting in the present condition.

She explained that weather patterns were no longer predictable. And because the land cover had been destroyed, rain water ran down bare gulleys and across tree-less plains, gathering into voluminous quantities that formed the dreaded floods that swept away people, animals and property.

She told them many people had moved into forests, cutting down trees to make timber and fencing posts. There were charcoal mounds everywhere, their chocking smoke billowing into the sky, abetting the pollution of the atmosphere and destroying the environment. River banks and water catchment areas were cleared and cultivated, loosening the soil that was eventually swept into the gulleys when it rained.

The worst offenders, she said, were large scale farms such as Olmakarr and Olkarsiss, who cleared tens of thousands of acres of forest land. Over the years, their odious deeds had created animal and human conflicts for which the pastoralists had to bear the brunt.

Unless the trend was reversed, she warned, their herds would completely vanish from the earth's surface, for there would be no pastures to support their lives.

She talked of the urgent need for all people to immediately vacate forests and the need for a programme of afforestation. If trees were planted and nurtured to maturity, and human interference curbed the land would heal and the environment restored.

Norpisia sat with a group of excited men and women listening attentively to the speech made by the prophetess. Occasionally, the people laughed, shouted and sometimes wailed, not out of distress, but because it was their most poignant way of responding to Sein's message.

She looked at the people who came to listen to the prophetess and noticed that they had all spruced themselves in their Sunday best: men in trousers and brightly coloured shirts, others in colourful blankets and clean shaven heads, some with bead ornaments around their necks and dangling from their extended ear-lobes.

There were women in cotton dresses, their heads tied up in bright flower-patterned headscarves. Other women who scorned the imported fashions had shaved heads, adorned their ears with bead ornaments, wrapped their bodies in bright *lesos*, and bedecked their necks with colourful necklaces.

Norpisia glanced at Kedoki. He was sitting still, his body tense with a strange expression on his face. He appeared nervous about something and she wondered what it was. She learnt later that people had told the prophetess that he, his wife and two other men had mysteriously arrived in Olmakarr farm and found favour with Barnoti. The people thought Barnoti was using them to sanitize his odious activities at Olmakarr farm by portraying himself as a converted conservationist. When Kedoki was asked to explain how they got into Olmakarr farm, he was happy to do so.

"It is a long story," he said taking a deep breath. He cleared his throat and thought about how to begin. He explained how, about ten years earlier, he left his home at Nkararo in Olorukoti, in search of green pastures. How they were attacked by bandits who killed his brother and his sister and stole forty heads of cattle. Left alone with a large herd of animals, he did not know what to do. It was then when the idea of looking for a wife to help him drive the cattle, dawned on him.

Kedoki, to the amazement of the crowd narrated his and his wife's experiences throughout the journey to Olmakarr farm. Danger had lurked everywhere with crocodiles waiting to rip off those who crossed the rivers, and trumpeting giant elephants hurtling down hills like cannons. Kedoki praised Norpisia for her unrivaled knowledge of herbs.

"Your knowledge of herbs is amazing," commented Sein, with ardent curiosity. "May you kindly tell us how you acquired it."

Norpisia was elated when Sein talked to her, for that was the opportunity she yearned for. She had wanted to tell Sein about the dreams she had on the conflict between wild animals and human beings; about the four wildebeests that she saved from imminent death; and about her secret wish, one she had not even told Kedoki. Yes, she wanted to tell her that when her baby boy, Kinyamal, grew up, she wanted him to become a game warden. She wanted him to fulfill her grandmother's wish that she herself could not fulfill.

"I was partly brought up by my grandmother," she explained. "She was an *Enkoiboni*, a medicine woman and a healer who introduced me to herbs and healing when I was very young."

She explained in detail how she moved to her grandmother's home following a bandit attack that also killed her brother and her sister. Her grandmother took her to the forest when she went to fetch roots, barks and leaves for her concoctions. She taught her the names of the herbs and their medicinal value. She was a witness as her grandmother treated many patients who consulted and sought treatment from her.

She also explained how other relatives were asked to train her in self-defence, self-reliance and the use of weapons particularly spears, bows, arrows and knobkerries. The women present were confounded to hear that a young woman was taught to handle weapons.

On the contrary, it was not only women who were confounded by Norpisia's testimony but men too were equally enthralled. The prophetess was mesmerized. For the first time, Kedoki realized that Norpisia was a good storyteller. Although he knew her story well, he was nevertheless drawn to the refreshing way she rendered it. She was clear and precise with exemplary word choice, accompanied by evocative gestures. She revealed how she was trained to mimic birds and animal sounds and how she eventually managed to imitate them with such finesse that even the birds and the animals could not tell the difference between the mimicked sound and that which was their own.

Finally, she divulged her grandmother's wish that she joins wild animals to fight human beings who destroyed their habitat. When Sein heard about the four wildebeests in their herd, she was not only surprised, but it fired her imagination to know more about Norpisia. Who was she and was there something peculiar about her? Sein vowed to find out.

When the meeting ended, Sein sought Norpisia, took her aside, and had a woman-to-woman tête-à-tête. Sein told Norpisia of her admiration of her steadfastness to fulfil her grandmother's wish. She reiterated that this resonated well with the wish of so many other people who wanted the destruction of the forest immediately halted, and the planting of trees hastened. She hoped that this would naturally help the return of the wild animals to their habitat and minimize human and animal conflict. Sein promised to visit Norpisia and have a look at her wildebeests.

Norpisia expressed delight at meeting the prophetess, whom she greatly admired. Just before they parted, Kedoki joined them. He wanted to know the opinion of the prophetess on certain gases said to be emitted by cattle and which polluted the environment. For the first time, Norpisia and Kedoki saw the prophetess laugh uproariously.

"If we plant trees and revive our environment," she said still roaring with laughter, "we shall then talk about those gases."

With that Norpisia and Kedoki went back to Olmakarr farm buoyed up by Sein's words. They promised to play their role in resuscitating the environment. There was renewed hope that as long as they had, in their midst, such altruistic people as Sein, the environment would be restored, the land healed and the collective soul of the people re-energised.

CHAPTER 16

Norpisia and Kedoki, being guests on a farm owned by one of those who were being criticized for encroaching on forest land, should have envisaged the consequences of attending a meeting called by Sein.

Barnoti knew of the meeting. The place where trees were planted was a symbol of things to come. According to him, those events were planned and orchestrated by the devious prophetess. He also felt betrayed. He regarded it as the height of utter foolishness, that a bunch of nomads, some of whom he had rescued from the brink of a catastrophe, would turn up in a meeting presided over by the activist. When Norpisia and Kedoki arrived back from the meeting, they found Salaash, waiting for them at the workers camp.

"How are you, my friends?" he greeted them happily. "How was the meeting?"

"We are fine and the meeting was lively," responded Kedoki.

Salaash informed them he had been sent to deliver a message to them. He said Barnoti wanted them to move out of Olmakarr farm because their cattle had exhausted the grass on the paddocks they were allocated. He suggested that they could try their luck at the Olkarsis farm. With that they knew their fate had been sealed.

Left on their own, Kedoki, Lembarta and Masintet recalled the wisdom in Norpisia quoting the founder who said someone else's milk-cow dried up at midday. They knew what they had feared had befallen them. Without much ado, they immediately embarked on planning and strategising on moving out of Olmakarr farm the following morning.

At daybreak, the following day Kedoki, Lembarta, Masintet and Norpisia thanked Barnoti for his hospitality and they swiftly drove their animals including the four wildebeests towards the west. They were headed for Eorr-Narasha, the home of Lembarta and Masintet.

The drought was still severe and the heat unbearable. As the sun rose higher in the sky, it struck the plains with such intensity, that shimmering heat waves could be seen rising from the earth. Sweat gleamed on the faces of the men as they ran back and forth controlling the movement of the herd. Norpisia, who was carrying her baby on her back, plodded along listlessly. The dogs' tongues lolled out of their mouths pathetically.

They rested briefly during the hottest hours of the day. Only the stunted *Iluaa*, grew in the area and could not offer them shade. In the evening when the sun began to dip, they began to look for a suitable place to camp for the night. Upon finding one, they set up their simple camp in the twilight. They drove their herd into the enclosure, and after ascertaining that the animals were all within the kraal, they stood in the midst of the cattle and looked across the distant plains. They discussed the changing circumstances of their lives. They feared that the condition of their cattle would rapidly deteriorate now that the grass, the water and the salt licks they were used to at Olmakarr farm were no more. Later on, they went to Norpisia's olngoborr, where they ravenously ate the *olpurda*.

The following day, they drove their animals across the Ngatet grassland. They saw a changing terrain ahead of them. The flat lowlands were giving way to rugged hills. As they started up toward those hills, they found that *Oleleshua* and *Olkiparrnyany* bushes grew on the lower slopes, while brush and tough wiry grass grew on the dry lee sides. In Norpisia's assessment, the land seemed more barren than she had imagined. She looked back from the heightened elevation of the hills and gained a new perspective of the land they had just crossed. The few *Ilopon* trees in the vicinity were bare of leaves; many animals grazed individually; and wildebeests were prevalent. They were gathering into large migratory herds and heading south. During the whole of that day, the bearded beasts with their short black horns moved over the rolling hills of the northern grassland in their thousands. The dust they raised rose to cast an obscuring blanket over the great moving mass, with the earth shaking, amidst the din of their grunts and bawls that rumbled like distant thunder.

Elephants were few, usually travelling in the opposite direction from the wildebeests. Once in a while, they sighted rhinoceroses, a rare phenomenon in that part of the country.

On their third night in the wilderness, Kedoki, lay beside Norpisia wondering if she had fallen asleep. Then she revealed her thoughts.

"We have now been travelling for the last three years," she said quietly. "We have come a long way, haven't we?"

"Yes, we have come a long way," he replied, a little guarded in his answer. He shifted to his side and raised up one arm so he could see her and the sleeping baby. "But we are still a long way from Nkararo, my village at Olorukoti. Are you tired of travelling?"

"A little. It is also tough for the baby," she said concernedly. "Little Kinyamal and I would like to rest for a while. Then we shall be ready to travel again. I didn't know this country was so big. Shall we ever get to your home?"

"The wise said home is never far for one who is still alive," he answered smiling, trying to up-lift her low spirits. "We are not far from Eorr-Narasha, the home of Lembarta and Masintet. When we get there, you will rest before we start our journey again."

Kedoki looked at her glowing face, feeling great love for the woman and her baby lying beside him. He was worried about her talk regarding the journey to Nkararo, for it made him think about the long way ahead before they got to his home. It was evident to Norpisia that after meeting the prophetess, life would never be the same again. Now that they had moved from Olmakarr farm, she wondered whether they would ever meet again.

Norpisia woke up before dawn the following day, for she was an early riser. She left the baby sleeping next to his father, went into the cattle enclosure to milk the cows, before preparing the milk and serving Lembarta, Masintet and Kedoki with steaming mugs. The pre-dawn sunlight spread slowly, reflecting a rosy glow in the east. Birds twittered, chirruped and sang excitedly on the acacia trees.

Before they drove their animals out, several morans clad in *shukas* carrying their long spears were seen in the distance. A number of them wore ceremonial headgear made of lion manes or ostrich plumes. Anxiety gripped Kedoki, Lembarta and Masintet who quickly held their weapons, ready for any eventuality. Norpisia scooped her baby and hastily retreated into her *Olngoborr*. One of the morans pulled back his ceremonial headgear and walked toward the three men who jerked their weapons with sudden apprehension.

"Ah, these are our two brothers," the young man told his companions, pointing at Lembarta and Masinttet. He grinned broadly and said, "It is me Lenjirr."

Lembarta looked at him closely and grinned "Lenjirr my brother! Is that you?"

The other young men came closer and greeted their seniors respectfully.

"Ara Kedoki!" Masintet said motioning Kedoki to come over. "This is Lenjirr our younger brother. He follows Lembarta." And turning to the young man he said, "This is Kedoki the man we went out to rescue in the wilderness."

Lenjirr introduced his friends and explained that they were on their way from a festival at a neighbouring village. They were heading home. Masintet sent them to tell the villagers they were on their way home.

Encouraged by the news that they were about to arrive, Norpisia marshaled all her reserved strength and walked energetically. The low, rolling plains gave way to steep hills and *Ilkinye* trees appeared among the brush. Then the wood of *Olpalagilagi* and *Oiti* with *Olgirgirri* intermixed forming an impregnable undergrowth. At the lower elevations, the region resembled the wooded hills they had already travelled through.

As they drove their animals in the wooded hillsides, Norpisia could almost believe she had been there before, if she hadn't known better. Everything seemed so familiar: the trees, the bushes, the slopes and the vegetation on the land. For an unknown reason, she kept hope of recognising a familiar landmark. She later realized that her familiarity stemmed from the resemblance of the terrain around her home at Olomuruti.

Later in the evening, Lembarta and his brother Masintet were proud to be back home, each driving his own ten cows, some of them leading their calves. Masintet was particularly eager to show off his homestead to Norpisia and Kedoki. He waited patiently outside the homestead for the two to absorb their dramatic entry to his home. Many people, men, women and children came out to welcome them. There were jovial shouts and excited exchanges of greetings. Some women cried with

178

joy while old men spat blessings on the faces of Lembarta and Masintet. There were frenzied celebrations, especially by the youth and women and muted excited admiration from old men, when they saw the cattle.

This exuberant reception, with dance and song overwhelmed and humbled Norpisia and Kedoki. Norpisia had not seen people overflowing with such life and excitement before.

When Ngoto Lesiamin, Masintet's wife, finally turned up leading her three children, to greet the visitors, she was confounded by the reaction of her husband. When she proffered her hand limply as she always did when greeting her husband, he let go her hand and reached up and gave her a hug instead. He bent over impulsively, picked the slender woman up and gave her a proper embrace. Slightly disconcerted, she looked up into his face with surprise: Her tall, handsome man had changed. She did not recall him being so spontaneous in demonstrating his affections in the past. When he finally put her down, she studied the man and woman he had brought along and wondered whether his change had anything to do with those two strangers. She and Norpisia had an immediate liking for one another. She took her into her house and from then hence forth, it was as if Norpisia had found a lost sister. The two were inseparable.

In a few days, Lembarta, Masintet and a few men from the village helped Kedoki to establish his temporary homestead. They cut thorn bushes and constructed a cattle enclosure. Within it, women helped Norpisia to erect her first semi-permanent house. Kedoki slaughtered a fat ram for the women as they celebrated the arrival of a young woman with an inexhaustible energy.

A few days after their arrival, Masintet approached Kedoki with a request. He had learnt that his mother, Ngoto Resiato, had been bitten by a crocodile as she fetched water at the river and that she was grievously wounded.

Having been a witness to Norpisia's knowledge of herbs, Masintet requested her to look at his mother's injured arm. Norpisia readily accepted to help.

Masintet and Kedoki accompanied her to Ngoto Resiato's house. In the dim light, Norpisia could just make out a woman reclining on a bed. Masintet knelt down and softly called his mother. The old woman opened her eyes, and her son bent over and put his hand on her forehead. It was apparent that the old woman was in great pain. Her eyes were glazed, her face ashen and flushed with fever. Even from where she stood, Norpisia could see that beneath the light blanket that covered her body, between the shoulder and elbow, her arm was bent in a grotesque angle.

"Mother, I have brought visitors to greet you," Masintet told her quietly. "Would you like to see them?"

"Visitors? Who are they?" She asked, slightly lifting her head to look at Kedoki who was also kneeling next to Masintet.

"It is Kedoki," Masintet answered slowly, speaking

like one who was talking to a small child. "I don't know whether you remember him, but he stayed with us some years back on his way to the north."

"Ah! Yes, I do remember him now," she said weakly, her sunken eyes lighting up with a flicker of recognition. "He was from Nkararo at Olorukoti, if my memory still serves me well."

Kedoki almost winced at the pain he saw etched on her face. "And he brought his wife with him," Masintet whispered tearfully. "Her name is Norpisia." He beckoned Norpisia to come closer to the bed.

"She is a medicine woman and a healer and she would like to examine your arm."

"Let me see your arm," Norpisia said as she uncovered the arm. The crocodile had nearly amputated the arm at the elbow. The wound had been cleaned and it was healing. However, the arm was swollen and the bone protruded beneath the skin at an odd angle. Norpisia felt the arm, trying to be as gentle as she could. The old woman winced in pain.

"I will try the much I can to treat your arm," Norpisia told the old woman. "I must, however, tell you my prescription shall be extremely painful and the healing process slow. But I believe you will be fully recovered and be able to use your arm again."

Norpisia asked Kedoki and Masintet to leave the room as she embarked on examining the old woman more closely. Her thoughts were drawn back to the time she lived with her grandmother. She recalled the intensive training she received from her. She remembered how she thoroughly examined her patients several times before deciding the mode of treatment or herbs she would use. Her grandmother cautioned relatives of the patients not to expect miracles, reminding them to accept that anything could happen in the course of treatment. She always emphasized that, it was *Enkai-Narok* who healed while death was caused by *Enkai-Nanyokie*, and the two were doled out without any consultation.

Norpisia concluded that her injuries were not life threatening. She was, however, going to use strong herbal medicine to numb her muscles in order to straighten and re-align the bones of her arm. When Norpisia explained everything in detail to the old woman's family, the youngest son, Lenjirr, was sceptical. He argued that his mother was not to be subjected to any treatment that could likely put her life at risk. When they could not agree on what to do they all trooped back to the old woman's house to consult her.

"*Yeiyo*," Lenjirr called his mother fondly, "May be you should not take the risk and accept this treatment. I don't want to lose you."

The old woman looked at her youngest child with loving kindness. "*Lenjirr Lai Lanyorr,*" she called out in the most loving tone. "There are not many days left in my life. If I had a choice, I would not like to spend those few remaining days in pain and carrying a useless arm. However, if this young woman can help to treat me, let her try. If it doesn't work, we shall all know we tried our

182

best. If I die in the process, that will be alright, for the old adage says an arrow does not miss a person destined to die."

Lenjirr sat on the bed beside his mother, held her good hand, looked into her face, and saw the determination in her eyes. He turned, looked around the room, and his stare settled on Norpisia.

"You have been honest with all of us," he told Norpisia arrogantly. "Now it is my turn to be honest with you. I will not hold it against you if your concoctions do not work. But I must warn you that if my mother dies, I don't care what your husband will do to me: I'll make sure that my spear goes through your rib-cage!"

There followed a deafening silence in the room.

"I'll do it," Norpisia said finally. "And bear whatever consequences!"

Kedoki was rather disappointed. As soon as they were in the safety of their house, he told Norpisia he did not think it right to put her life on the line. But Norpisia would not hear of it. She told her husband it was for such cases, as Resiato's mother that her grandmother trained her in traditional medicine. She reasoned that the old woman's injury was not as bad as the one inflicted by the cattle rustlers on Kedoki which she successfully treated.

In the afternoon of the following day, Norpisia took her new friend, Ngoto Lesiamin, Masintet's wife, and headed to the forest. Ngoto Lesiamin showed Norpisia around and then led her right into the dense forest. Norpisia moved from one bush to another digging up

183

roots, plucking leaves and cutting tree barks. Soon, she had a bag full of assorted roots, leaves, berries, barks and twigs. When she got home, she boiled several concoctions and put them into calabashes, before commencing the treatment.

The old woman thought she saw a painful look flash across the young woman's face as she got up and went to the fire to start mixing the herbal medicine. She knew her son had hurt her with his infuriating threats. She had had a long talk with him in which she rebuked and scolded him severely for his conduct.

After treating the old woman for many weeks, Norpisia observed that she was getting better. And slowly, the arm began to heal and soon she was using it to lift light things. When villagers saw the progress, Norpisi'a house was inundated with a mass of sickly people, seeking treatment of various kinds of ailments. Norpisia did not disappoint them. Beside treatment, she taught women simple prescriptions that they would give to their infants to forestall colds and fevers.

"Did you sleep well, *Yeiyo?*" Norpisia asked the old woman several months later.

"I am feeling better than I have ever felt since I was bitten by the crocodile," she answered with a fond look at Norpisia.

As Norpisia brought changes in the lives of the people of Eorr-Narasha village, she did not forget the promise she made to the prophetess. She had promised that she would play her role, however small, to restore the depleted forests and resuscitate the degraded environment.

CHAPTER 17

Norpisia had another nightmare that jolted her awake. She quickly sat up on the bed and turned to touch the face of her baby ensuring that he was sleeping peacefully. It was in the course of confirming that the baby was all right that she realized that her hands were shaking. Her entire body was soaked in sweat. She gently shook Kedoki who woke up with a start. It was then that they heard a commotion outside. A donkey neighed, they heard hooves stamping, and then a stampede. A bull bellowed and dogs barked fiercely. When they heard a dog snarl and yelp in pain, they threw off their blankets and rushed out.

It was dark though a silver moon shed a dim light. Inside the cattle enclosure, agitated cattle milled around, while bulls pawed and trampled on heavily. Kedoki quickly surveyed the cattle enclosure and with an expert eye, confirmed that none of his cattle were missing. The thorn fence that surrounded the cattle enclosure was intact. But outside the kraal, hundreds of wildebeests were moving away. It occurred to him that there was need to check on their four wildebeests. They were not in the cattle enclosure. They were gone: The wildebeests had come to fetch their own.

On learning that the wildebeests of which she was so fond of were gone, Norpisia was devastated. At first, she did not believe it. She moved from one group of cattle to the other, ascertaining that they were not hiding in their midst; she ran around the perimeter thorn fence, checking for a crack through which they may have passed. Suddenly, she tripped on an exposed root and fell heavily on the ground. Kedoki heard her fall and rushed toward her in the dark.

"*Ngoto Kinyamal!*" he called her using her newly acquired name. "Are you all right?"

"I am alright," she answered in a hoarse voice, trying to catch her breath. "My foot was caught under the creeping roots of *Olkiarr-enkure* plant."

"Get up my dear," he told her fondly, giving her his hand for support. "The wise said an elephant is felled by a grass creeper!"

When they heard the sound of the wildebeests racing off into the night, Norpisia pulled herself up and followed her husband. They ran toward the herd of wildebeests, but they were all gone.

"My beloved *Inkati* are gone!" she cried and started after the wildebeests, stumbling through the woods in the dark. "I must get them back by all means!"

Kedoki quickly followed and caught up with her in a few strides.

"*Ngoto Kinyamal* wait!" he called after her. "We can't follow the beasts right now. It is dark."

"But we have to get them back," she said anxiously. "We

187

have to get them before they go far."

"We will follow them and bring them back in the morning," Kedoki told her re-assuringly. "We shall see their tracks and follow them. I promise you, I will bring them back."

"Oh, my husband, it would be a shame if we lose the four beasts," she said breaking down into tears. 'You were there when I told the prophetess about the wildebeests. She said she would soon come to see them. What shall we tell her if she were to come and find them gone? She may think I made up the story."

"That will not happen," he told her encouragingly. "I am certain we shall bring them back into our herd."

As they walked back into the cattle enclosure, they came across a dead dog. Its rib-cage was severed. They concluded that it must have been trampled on by the wildebeests.

When they got back in the house, Norpisia went straight to check on her baby. She then stirred up the fire and boiled some milk. She served her husband and took some herself.

While they drank their milk, Norpisia told her husband about her nightmare. She had a dream in which she was walking through a barren wilderness. There were bare boulders everywhere without a single tree in sight. Suddenly, there appeared a stretch of grassy land, lush and green. Thereafter; there appeared four wildebeests and four cows, all fighting for the limited green grass on the dry patch of land. There was a lioness that led its two cubs stealthily towards the tussling animals.

She observed closely to see whether the lioness would hunt down a wildebeest or a milk cow. As she looked, the lioness turned into a woman. She strained to see who it was, and she was startled to see her grandmother stepping out of the shadows. She motioned her on, urging her to hurry and follow her, before she disappeared behind a big boulder. Norpisia followed her grandmother and found her standing beside a heap of tree seedlings. Beside the seedlings were the four cows and four wildebeests, hungry and emaciated. The eight animals were now threatening to eat up the seedlings in the heap. Her grandmother urged her to pick the seedlings and plant them. She was bending to pick up the seedlings when a devilish man appeared, grabbed them and took off. She ran after him, and came to a place where the path forked. She was greatly confused. She was still undecided over which path to take when her grandmother appeared again, rebuking and scolding her severely, she urged her to plant the seedlings immediately. It was then that she woke up with a start.

Kedoki listened; wondering what the dream portended. He had learnt over the years not to brush her dreams away.

Norpisia did not fall asleep again after that commotion. She turned and tossed several times on her bed, consumed by the nightmare and the disappearance of her beloved wildebeests.

The moment the sky lit up, she was up. She stirred

the embers on the fire, took her calabash, went into the cattle enclosure and began milking.

When she got back into the house, her husband was up and getting ready for the task ahead. Norpisia handed him his calabash of milk, went to Ngoto Lesiamin's house and requested her to look after her baby. Kedoki on the other hand, requested Lembarta to drive his herd of cattle to the pastures for the day.

"Look, Ngoto Kinyamal," Kedoki told Norpisia as he bent down to examine the imprint of wildebeests' hooves. "Hundreds of wildebeests must have been here last night."

"You were right when you said it would be easy to track them in the morning." Norpisia said quietly.

They were near the edge of the small woods, and she could see far into the distance across the open grassy plain, however, there was no single wildebeest in sight.

They followed the trail toward the eastern dry plains, before the trucks inexplicably changed direction. It was not until mid afternoon that they finally caught up with the wildebeests. As they drew nearer, Norpisia thought she had a glimpse of the brand marks on the coat of one of the wildebeests, but she wasn't sure. There were too many other wildebeests on the move making it impossible to distinguish her own. When they got nearer, the wind carried their scent to the herd, and they scampered away.

Kedoki thought the herd's behaviour suggested the presence of lions or poachers in the vicinity. He kept

190

his thoughts to himself for he did not want to upset Norpisia any further. As Norpisia and Kedoki moved on, they noticed that the ground had begun to slope downward. The terrain had become rugged and grass became sparse. The waters of river Enkipai sparkled below a plateau that was on top of a hill that Kedoki and his group had skirted on their way to the Eorr-Narasha village. The smaller river, called *Inkiito* that passed near the village, hugged the hill's eastern face before joining the huge Enkipai river.

When the animals reached the plain, they settled again and started to graze steadily.

"My husband, look!" Norpisia cried excitedly, pointing at a group of wildebeests. "There they are!"

"How can you be sure they are the ones?" Asked Kedoki doubtfully. "All those beasts look the same to me."

Just then, the entire herd turned and headed toward the river and Norpisia lost sight of her wildebeests. Although disappointed, they followed them. At the riverside, the beasts grazed contentedly, giving Kedoki and Norpisia a chance to observe them from a close range. Norpisia had just identified her four wildebeests that stood in a group, when Kedoki nudged her pointing at a spot under the trees a few metres from where they stood. Camouflaged under foliage in the trees were faces of four people who had been watching them for some time. Kedoki confirmed his earlier feeling that the wildebeests were either being hunted by poachers or stalking lions. They were about to retreat into the bushes when a woman emerged out of the shadows. Under the bright noon sunshine, Kedoki and Norpisia immediately recognized the woman. Sein, the prophetess, was the last person they expected to see in the wilderness. Sein did not appear baffled by the presence of Norpisia and Kedoki. With a broad smile, she swiftly moved towards Norpisia with her arms outstretched.

"What a surprise to see you here, Norpisia," Sein hugged her tightly. "What are the two of you doing out here in the bush?"

Norpisia explained that they were in pursuit of their four wildebeests. As they talked, the four beasts moved from the herd and stood a few metres away, facing Norpisia and the rest. Norpisia whistled and the four animals turned and looked at them.

"I told you," Norpisia told Kedoki happily. "They are the ones."

"What a wonderful sight!" Eddah Sein exclaimed in amazement. "I have not seen anything like that before."

Norpisia whistled again, and the four wildebeests started towards them. But before they moved closer, a large bull with a dark greyish coat, a silver mane and short thick horns, quickly overtook them. The three people who Sein left behind under the trees, came out into the open, driven by curiosity to watch the unfolding scenario.

"What are we going to do now?" Norpisia asked Kedoki forlornly. "It is apparent that the bulls won't let our wildebeests go."

"Why don't you call them as you always did when

giving them milk?" Kedoki suggested.

Norpisia whistled in the manner she always did to them every morning. They always came to her running and nuzzled up against her, searching for their milk bottle, the *Esiorog*.

"Iinkati laainei, wootu! " she called them out repeatedly.

They were all astonished to see the four wildebeests moving closer to Norpisia, swishing their short wiry and brownish tails as they nuzzled against her hand.

"Wootu, iinkati laainei! " she kept on calling them, as she touched their heads to calm and reassure them.

The rest of the herd watched the unfolding scene with nervous interest. From a safe distance, they bellowed and grunted, staring at the four wildebeests interacting with human beings. Suddenly, the wild animals began to look unsettled. They looked up and about them. Norpisia had a hunch that something was amiss. She turned around to look at Kedoki. He also looked perturbed. From a distance, they spotted a pride of lions stealthily stalking the beasts. Suddenly, there was a stampede and the entire herd scampered away. Norpisia had a hard time calming her four wildebeests. Fortunately, the lions disappeared into the bushes in pursuit of their prey.

Sein introduced her companions to Norpisia and Kedoki. She and her team were on a mission to organize the itinerary of a group of tourists taking part in an expedition to photograph the migration of wildebeests crossing the Enkipai river. When one of the three men noticed the brand marks on the backs of the four wildebeests, he jokingly suggested that the four animals could be coaxed to participate in future annual rituals and could be made part of the itinerary. Sein said she could easily find a sponsor who would take up the venture as a sporting activity as well as a tourist attraction. Jokingly, she said the sports could be called 'Spot Norpisia's branded beasts!'

Indeed, within a year, Sein had developed the idea and turned the nondescript joke that was mooted at the riverside, into a sport and business venture that had to be booked several months in advance, enabling both Kedoki and Norpisia to earn some money.

When Kedoki told Sein that they were thrown out of Olmakarr farm soon after attending her meeting, she promised that soon the owners of Olmakarr and Olkarsiss farms would be evicted by people opposed to the continued destruction of the environment. Before she departed, she promised to visit Eorr-Narasha village within the next three months and review progress on resuscitation of the environment.

As they drove the four wildebeests back to Eorr-Narasha village, Norpisia was in a contemplative mood. In contrast, Kedoki seemed to be in a particularly good mood. The events of that afternoon appeared to have rejuvenated them. The recovery of their lost wildebeests and the dramatic meeting with Sein, breathed new life into their souls. And, perhaps because of the dream she had had the night before, she now took keen interest in every tree seedling that she came across. She was particularly interested in plants near Enkipai river and in the adjacent grasslands.

Kedoki felt relieved that they had recovered the four wildebeests. However, he was becoming increasingly worried by the way his wife appeared to be weighed down by matters that had nothing to do with their core business of rearing cattle. Although he did not grudge her association with the prophetess, he was somehow getting alarmed at the influence the prophetess was exerting on her. They needed to get out of Eorr-Narasha village to Nkararo soon.

When they got home, a women delegation was waiting for Norpisia at the entrance of their homestead. One of the delegates told Norpisia they had come to ask her to lead them in the tree planting project that they envisaged to undertake.

Kedoki knew they were ensnared. Their journey to Nkararo that he thought would commence soon, had to be delayed.

CHAPTER 18

When word reached Sein, that women had nominated Norpisia to lead them in conserving the environment, she knew they had made the right choice. On the few occasions they had met, Sein was convinced that Norpisia was a born-leader. She could successfully lead her community in tackling some of the issues that had contributed to the degradation of the environment.

True to Sein's appraisal, when Norpisia was asked by the womenfolk to spearhead the resuscitation of the environment, she accepted the challenge wholeheartedly and immediately embarked on afforestation. With the help of Eorr-Narasha elders, she picked on a desolate area that was once a dense forest. Other than the tough wiry grass known as *olmagutian* that survived the drought, the only other woody vegetation visible in that area was the thorny brush that could withstand the arid heat. An occasional thin-branched *oleleshua* with its tiny woolly white flowers, or the stunted *Olaimurunyai* with its black round berries and sharp thorns, dotted the landscape. Only a few, bushy *Olobaai* shrubs, could be seen on the hillside. The most prevalent vegetation was the tripod thorn, *Ilaimerrerruak*, that made it impossible for one to walk over the terrain barefooted.

After identifying the area to be reforested, Norpisia led women in digging holes of the right depth into which they were to plant tree seedlings. Each woman carried a water container. Afterwards, Norpisia led the women to the distance hill where the only surviving forest was located. Before them was a long line of huge and tall trees. The moment they stepped within the shade of the high canopy of leaves, they found themselves enclosed in a deep, dense, mixed forest of huge hardwood trees and the evergreen undergrowth. It was dark in there and it took a few moments before their eyes adjusted to the dim light in the silent forest. They could immediately feel the cool damp air and the smell of the decaying leaves. Thick moss covered the ground in a thick green carpet and climbed over boulders. It spread over the rounded shapes of ancient trees that had long fallen, and circled disintegrating stumps. The women walked on the forest floor that was littered with the remnants of rotting vegetation, regenerating new life.

From the mossy rotting logs, the women found sprouting seedlings of all kinds and a variety of saplings, struggling to find a place in the sun. Quickly, they began to uproot them carefully, putting them in their bags.

They kept moving deeper and deeper into the forest as they collected the seedlings and saplings.

By the time they got home, the moon was high in

the sky and each one of them was happy to be safe, with a bag full of tree seedlings and saplings.

The following morning after milking, the women carried their tree seedling to the area that they had prepared, planted and watered them. For the next three months, they repeated the exercise until the whole planted section was with new seedlings.

Eorr-Narasha's women took up the tree planting project so enthusiastically that even Sein, was delighted. Every time she visited the village, she congratulated Norpisia for her exemplary leadership qualities. Although the project was replicated in many villages across the country, it was not so successful anywhere as it was in Eorr-Narasha. Sein was enthralled when Norpisia led her through an exclusive area where she had established a beautiful botanical garden, within the growing forest, with all kinds of herbs which the villagers would later use to treat their ailments.

Encouraged by women's interest in resuscitating the environment, Sein, in collaboration with other conservationists, initiated an incentive scheme that immediately revolutionized tree planting and rehabilitation of the degraded environment among the pastoralist communities. Even the menfolk who initially had shown little interest in the exercise, were now seen in long queues, receiving and planting tree seedlings. The scheme was named *Sheep for Trees Initiative*. This was meant to encourage villagers to plant more trees. For every fifty tree-seedlings planted and protected from animals, one was rewarded with a sheep.

That did the trick and the response was encouraging. Sein and other conservationists distributed thousands of exotic tree seedlings. At the same time, the rain came down in a steady deluge, as though the heavens were in some league with the project.

A few weeks before the date set to reward those conservationists whose tree-seedlings had survived, Sein visited Norpisia and accompanied her on a tour of the exotic tree plantation. They walked to the top of a ridge and looked out over it unto a wide plateau that dropped down gently and then extended to a long distant level ground. As far as they could see, a coniferous forest of dark green cypress and pine trees dominated the plateau. The *Inkiito* river that was drying up, now looked robust and rumbled on with cascading waters, its banks flourishing with deep, green undergrowth. Rising up beyond the tableland, was the breathtaking vista of *Oldonyo-Orasha* mountain.

On that beautiful sunny afternoon, Norpisia looked at the imposing feature which seemed so close that she felt she could almost reach and touch it. The sun behind them illuminated the colours and shapes of the mountain rocks, the vegetation around it and contrasted it with the now upcoming dense forest that the *Eorr-Narasha* people had planted and nurtured to maturity. While they watched, the sun and the cascading waters of *Inkiito* river created a glowing rainbow that straddled the mountain in a beautiful multi-coloured arc.

The two women gazed at the new look of the natural phenomenon in wonder, taking in the beauty and serenity of the created atmosphere. Norpisia wondered whether the rainbow was a symbol of something, whether it implied that the war with those who destroyed the environment, was finally being won. Sein on the other hand, noticed that the air she was breathing was deliciously cool and fresh.

As the conservationists enjoyed the beautiful scenery of the luxuriant forest and listened to the wind sighing, something was happening elsewhere. A group of young shepherds who had been temporarily employed to drive a flock of two thousand sheep to Eorr-Narasha village, were on their way. The young ewes, had been purchased from Olkarsiss and Olmakarr farms to reward the villagers who had nurtured their seedlings.

The shepherds drove the sheep across the plains stopping at every water source to let them drink. The shepherds camped in the afternoon to give them ample time to graze and rest. It took them a whole month to get to Eorr-Narasha village. On arrival, the sheep were in such good condition that those who saw them could hardly believe they had been trekking for a month.

The following morning was the day the villagers were meant to be rewarded. The entire village was there, with Lembarta and Masintet taking charge of the impending ceremony. Sein, the prophetess was there too, looking comfortable and relaxed. Norpisia was so pleased and went straight to embrace her. She had come with colleagues who were warmly received.

The village women had come out in multitudes. Most wore their best bright *lesos* and adorned themselves with exquisite multi-coloured beads. Even old Ngoto Rasiato, came out wearing her red *shukas*, swinging her arm, a testimony that Norpisia's treatment had worked. Ngoto Lesiamin was busy trying to quiet Norpisia's Kinyamal and her own child, who would not obey her orders.

Village elders were there too, with multi-coloured blankets, and fly-whisks. Also present were men and women from nearby villages who had come to witness the award ceremony.

Sein had bought a special ox that was slaughtered and roasted for the day. The throng of men, women and children chatted and laughed merrily as they feasted on large quantities of roasted, fried and boiled meat. Kedoki, tall and handsome, moved between clusters of men towering over them as he organized their sitting arrangement. Sein felt very much at ease, eating with the people and wiping her hands with velvety leaves of *Oleleshua*.

After the feast, Sein stood up, asked all those present to lift up their eyes and look across the valley, and see the pleasant view of the green forest. She reminded them that three years back, that area was badly ruined, like many other places across the country, where forests had been destroyed and the environment degraded. She congratulated Norpisia for spearheading the afforestation project. She pointed out that everyone could now see the benefit of a conserved environment. The air was fresh, and the water clean and cool. The weather patterns were stabilizing, and incidents of floods were becoming fewer. If people could only sustain the afforestation programmes, the country would revert back to a predictable weather pattern and the constant supply of grass for their animals all the year round. Even large land owners, like those who owned Olkarrsiss and Olmakarr farms, had now voluntarily surrendered the forest land that they had grabbed for reafforestation.

The people of Eorr-Narasha loved livestock so much that when the time came to reward those who had planted and nurtured tree-seedlings, the entire crowd broke into song and dance.

The distribution of the sheep according to the number of trees each villager had planted and nurtured, was an arduous but most delightful task. Sein had a list of names she had prepared earlier, the number of trees each planted, and the number of sheep to be handed over. For the first time in the history of Eorr-Narasha, women were way ahead of men in the number of livestock they brought into their homesteads. Most women earned more sheep than their men.

Norpisia earned fifty-five sheep while her husband, Kedoki earned thirty. Lembarta and his brother Masintet earned twenty-five sheep each, while Ngoto Lesiamin, Masintet's wife, got forty-five sheep. Even Ngoto Resiato, inspite of her incapacitation, earned herself five sheep.

At the end of the exercise, Norpisia felt fulfilled when she observed the warm camaraderie among the people milling around and congratulating one another for their achievements. But what was most gratifying to her, was Sein's approval of her actions and her husband's backing.

The following morning, Kedoki opened his eyes to the rumpled blanket on the empty place beside him on the bed. He pushed his blanket aside and sat up. Looking around, he realized he must have slept late. Norpisia was not in the house and so was his little boy, Kinyamal. The night before, she had talked about her dream to lead women to plant more trees. He had reminded her that they had to leave for their home at Nkararo before the rainy season began, and made it impossible to cross Ilkarian river.

Though they had not argued over it, Norpisia had indicated she did not want them to leave. She talked of the sick people who were on treatment, the medicinal herbs that she had planted in her botanical garden, of the need to assign the medicinal task to one villager whom she wanted to train. Kedoki felt that she wanted to stay in Eorr-Narasha, and wondered whether she was trying to delay their departure in the hope of forcing him to establish their permanent home there. She and Ngoto Lesiamin, Masintet's wife, had become very close friends and Norpisia would find it difficult to part with her. He also knew that everyone in the village seemed to like her very much. Although it pleased him, he feared that this would make their departure more difficult.

He had lain awake far into the night reflecting. He toyed with the idea of staying on for Norpisia's sake, but his mind refused to warm up to it; they would have to leave as soon as possible. He hoped to convince Norpisia.

For the next five days, the villagers tried in their own subtle ways to persuade Kedoki to change his mind with little success.

Soon, there was a flurry of activities as plans were made to bid them farewell. Masintet slaughtered a steer and offered it to the villagers to celebrate the marvelous time they had had together with Kedoki and Norpisia and how much they had contributed toward conserving the environment.

"Where is Norpisia?" Kedoki asked when he could not see her amongst the merry makers. "Has anybody seen my wife?"

"I am sure she will be here soon," answered Ngoto Resiato quietly. "She is with Ngoto Lesiamin. Those two have become inseparable of late. She was crying last night, wishing you could change your mind and stay. To tell you the truth, I'm sorry to see you go. Norpisia has done wonders here. I can never thank her sufficiently for having healed my arm. And how can Eorr-Narasha ever repay her for what she has done to restore our environment? We still need her here. Are you sure you don't want to change your mind?"

"You don't know how hard this decision has been to me," Kedoki said in a sorrowful voice. "You see, I have been away from my home for many years. Who knows what I'll find when I get there? I don't know whether my father and mother are still alive. I had a little sister who was very small when I left. She would be grown up now and would probably not remember me. But what I have always wanted to do, is to introduce Norpisia, to my parents, relatives and friends. Norpisia and I feel so close to everyone here, but as much as we would like to stay, home beckons. We have to go!"

When they had eaten, Masintet saw his wife Ngoto Lesiamin walking back from the field with Norpisia.

"My wife is soon going to be a medicine woman," he said pleasantly. "For the last few days there has been nothing else on her lips other than names of herbs and their uses."

"The knowledge Norpisia is sharing with Ngoto Lesiamin is her gift to Eorr-Narasha people," Ngoto Resiato said seriously.

"That reminds me, we have some gifts for you and Norpisia," Masintet chipped in as he rummaged through a leather bag. "We hope you will like them."

He took a wrapped item and handed it to his mother to present it to Norpisia.

"This is for you Norpisia," Ngoto Resiato offered the gift to Norpisia. "It is a gift to you by all the women of Eorr-Narasha for what you have done for all of us. I particularly thank you for healing me."

Norpisia, looking surprised, untied the cord and opened the soft tanned sheep-skin skirt, beautifully decorated with beads. She lifted it up and caught her breath.

It was the most beautiful *Olokesena* skirt she had ever seen.

"*Yeiyo-o-Resiato!*" Norpisia called out emotionally, putting down the garment and hugging the old woman passionately. "This is so beautiful. Truly I have never seen anything like it."

Norpisia looked at Kedoki and smiled in excitement.

Masintet put his hand into the leather bag again and pulled out two items. One was a shiny black knobkerry known as *oringa-orok* and a soft, grey woolly cloak made out of hyraxes skins sewn together into an outer garment called *enkila-oondeerri.* The two items were only given as gifts to persons who were highly respected in the community. The elders of Eorr-Narasha had found Kedoki a perfect measure to their expectation of a leader and elder.

"Thank you so much," Kedoki said excitedly, putting on the garment and taking up the knobkerry. He examined the items with wonder and reverence. He lifted the knobkerry and shifted it for balance in adoration. "These items mean a lot to me. I will always treasure them!"

The following morning, almost everyone in Eorr-Narasha had congregated outside the village to bid farewell to Norpisia, Kedoki and their child Kinyamal. Many of the people voiced their wish to walk along with them for a short distant. Their cattle, sheep, goats and donkeys had been separated from the village livestock. Even the four wildebeests were there too. Village elders began to drive them away from the village slowly.

"I won't be going far," Ngoto Resiato told Kedoki and Norpisia, tears streaming down her old wringled face. "I wish you could stay with us longer. All the same, I wish both of you a safe journey. Pass our greetings to your parents and the villagers there."

"Thank you, *yeiyo-o-Resiato,*" Norpisia said embracing the old woman with a hug. "We shall certainly need your blessings as we go through this last part of our journey."

"I want to thank you once again Kedoki, for bringing us your wife Norpisia," Ngoto Resiato said emotionally. "I don't even want to think about what would have happened to my arm had she not come."

"Life will never be the same again," said Ngoto Lesiamin, her eyes glistening with tears. "Norpisia, you have been my mentor. I will always remember you in my entire life. If you will excuse me, I would like to bid you farewell here. It won't be any easier for me to say goodbye out on the pastureland. Farewell good people!"

Those who did not wish to escort the Kedokis to the pastureland went back to the village. The others followed them for a short distant and then parted ways.

CHAPTER 19

To confirm what they had heard: that single-handedly, an environmentalist, Sein, had inspired, encouraged and assisted thousands of pastoralists to rehabilitate their environment, the leaders embarked on a countryside tour.

When they left in the morning, the leaders and their entourage headed for the Oldonyo-Orasha mountain passing through grasslands and driving through diverse woodlands teaming with wildlife. They did not travel far before they came across the expansive area where pastoralists had their first project of afforestation. The leaders observed that the trees the villagers planted were a wide assortment of indigenous varieties, such as *Iltepes, Ilera, Ilopon*, and *Ilpopong* among others.

The experts in the entourage explained to the leaders how ingenuously the indigenous people chose the varieties of tree seedlings they planted. They noted that the varieties depended on differences in climate, ground elevation, availability of water, or kinds of soils.

In the highlands of Shapaltarakua, Medungi and Ilpoldon, the leaders were amazed to see how dense the forests had grown. Evergreen trees that preferred slopes such as Ilpoldon, Ilpiripiri, Iloirraga, Iloirienito, Iltarakua and others soared into great heights as they competed for sunlight high up in the sky. Everywhere they went and every ridge they crossed, they were welcomed by clusters of *Iloururr* trees with their perfectly straight trunks. On slanting hillsides, where breaks in the leafy canopy allowed sunlight to penetrate to the ground, the undergrowth was luxuriant, with flowering *Ilkilenya* and other climbers often trailing down from the high branches of trees.

They crossed many flowing streams and rivers that were clothed with leafy stands of majestic *Ilama*, elegant *Iretet* and fragrant *Isinante*. Everywhere they looked they saw trees and more trees that gently swayed back and forth in the wind.

Not all villagers planted trees though. There was one village a few kilometers past Eorr-Narasha where its leader forbade his people from planting trees. He argued that trees had nothing to do with rain as it comes from the sky.

When the leaders and their entourage eventually trooped back into their familiar ground in town, they were well-informed. They appreciated the work done by the person they once vilified. They had warned her several times in the past to stop arrogating herself roles that had nothing to do with her. But her irrepressible spirit was unstoppable.

The following morning after the tour, Sein was summoned by the governor. She was informed that she had been nominated for an award in recognition of her tireless effort in the rehabilitation and conservation of the environment.

Sein told the governor and his officers that although she appreciated their nomination for an award, there were others who were more deserving than she. She informed them of one woman called Norpisia Kedoki, who she said deserved to be awarded the highest accolade for her services to her community. She was an inspirational leader who led her community in turning a desolate arid land that had hitherto been destroyed by charcoal burners, timber harvesters and expasionists into a dense green forest. She added that Norpisia had helped to reduce the human, animal conflict between them. Norpisia was also a herbalist. Her herbal medicine treated both human beings and livestock. Finally, she divulged that, Norpisia had reared wildebeests that had become an attraction to tourists and formed part of the tourist package that was marketed overseas.

The governor and his officers got interested in Norpisia and scheduled an interview with her. But they said they had very little time left before the awards were presented. If she was to be considered for possible nomination, Sein had to get her within the next three days. Sein was equal to the task as she did not think that was a difficult thing to achieve.

Very early the following morning, Sein's Suzuki four-wheeler was on its way out of Nakuru town, its nose pointed toward Eorr-Narasha, the red dust flying from under its wheels and its speedometer indicator flickering between eighty and a hundred. She had to bring Norpisia to Nakuru within two days as she had promised. She drove fast toward the shores of Lake Elementaita. The lake was an empty bed from which clouds of white dust rose up in the wind.

At noon, she crossed Enkipai river. She could see the majestic Oldonyo-Orasha mountain. She was not very far from Eorr-Narasha. If she found Norpisia at home, convinced her and her husband Kedoki to accompany her back to Nakuru, they might be there late that night. If that would be the case then she would have time to prepare them for the impending function. However, there were clouds gathering around the mountain, and that worried her. A tongue of forked lightning leapt from the huge flank of the mountain. She loved the rain for it invigorated the environment but she knew it could also very easily wreak havoc on a day like that.

"I can smell the rain," Sein thought aloud exultantly as the fresh, moisture-laden wind slapped her cheeks. A herd of Thomson's gazelle had smelt the rain, too, and were galloping madly across the grassland until they saw Sein's car. They halted to look at her, standing motionless except for their swinging tails. Beyond them a lone wildebeest stood sentinel, giving his silent, secret warning signal that danger lay ahead. Zebras cantered lazily past the lone wildebeest, and appeared unperturbed by the presence of Sein's vehicle. From far, she could see the storm blowing across the ridge where she thought Eorr-Narasha was. The narrow road that was nothing but two-wheel tracks with a high ridge of tufted grass between them, went on and on into the very heart of the Eorr-Narasha savannah land, through hills blackened by recent grass fires. Then she saw the forest, which Norpisia planted, on the wide, wind-swept plateau. About half an hour later, on the crest of a rise, she came straight into the storm she had seen earlier. The sky suddenly opened right on top of her vehicle. Thick balls of hail hit the roof and the windscreen. She stopped the vehicle, for it was impossible to see anything through the glass.

The storm was over as quickly as it had come, leaving the country washed and bright again. But when Sein resumed driving, she had to drive very carefully as the further she penetrated along the wretched track, the stickier the surface became.

She got to Eorr-Narasha and enquired the whereabouts of Norpisia and Kedoki. Her spirits sank. She was crest-fallen on learning that the couple left for Nkararo in Olorukoti, seven days earlier. Sein was siezed with panic as she had never experienced before. She explained to Lembarta and Masintet the reason why it was so important to find Norpisia, and the two men offered to accompany her hoping to find them before they crossed the treacherous river.

They were driving fast out of Eorr-Narasha village when the second storm caught up with them a few kilometres from the village. It was accompanied by gigantic thunder-claps followed by immense flashes of lightning that lit the sky. As the lightning flared and the thunder resounded, the three occupants of the vehicle trembled with fear. They drove for sometime but they were forced to stop near a village whose leader once discouraged his people from planting trees. They sat fearfully in the vehicle while the earth and heaven rocked with the fury of Enkai-Nanyokie.

The rain hurled into the dry river-beds, swirled into gullies, poured over the pasturelands, tearing at the soil, tugging at the tender roots of maize and wheat at the Olmakarr and Olkarrsiss farms. It formed rivulets into the Nkiito river below. The raging brown water, tore the weakest part of the river bank and overflowed the edges.

When the rain subsided, they resumed their journey toward Ilkarian river. Sein was getting desperate for it was getting late and she knew they were still far from their destination. The road was now atrociously wet and slippery and she found it difficult to control the vehicle as it swayed from side to side. She became furious with the weather and bit her lower underlip so hard that she tasted her own blood.

"I have got to find her," she kept on telling herself as she wrestled with the steering wheel. "I have got to. I must convince her to come with me. I must find a way of explaining to both of them that the trip to Nakuru is so important and so urgent that they must at once leave their livestock in the care of other people and follow me."

It was about three in the afternoon when they approached the low valley on which the Ilkarian river flowed. From their vantage point on the plateau of the open grassland above the broad valley with its wide, swiftly flowing river, they could see the terrain on the other side, across the valley. The foothills across the river were fractured with many ravines and gullies that were the result of the ravages of many years of flooding. As they rounded the shoulder of the plateau and drove down the slope, Sein was distraught and anxious when it started to rain again. Suddenly, a burst of lightning flashed, filling the valley with an instant brilliance. Then they drove out of the woods, and got into a clearing. She could now see the rolling clouds through the rain. Within a flash of a second, Sein's eyes dilated as she suddenly saw something that shocked her out of her wits. There right before them, in front of the vehicle, trees were moving as if on their own volition! She realized she had not noticed the rumble growing louder until she saw animals floating on water and heard distress sounds of lowing cows, bleating sheep and goats. She glanced back at Lembarta and Masintet and gasped. From the highlands the rain water had gathered into floods. Gathering momentum, the tumultuous water, abetted by the continuing deluge, raged down the steep hills with devastating force.

As they watched in horror, they saw the swift flooding water sweep away Kedoki's cattle, sheep, goats and donkeys. They witnessed the herd literally vanishing downstream. They could see Kedoki running up and down frantically, shunting wildly. His little boy,

Kinyamal, was on his shoulders, howling and crying his heart out. Norpisia was nowhere to be seen.

"Oh my God!" cried Sein as they jumped out of the vehicle and ran to the river bank, searching for Norpisia. Sein's eyes were tearful as she gazed at the swift flowing river. "God have mercy!" she cried out prayerfully.

CHAPTER 20

O n the day they left Eorr-Narasha for his home at Nkararo, Kedoki and Norpisia stood in a clearing that commanded a panoramic view of Oldonyo-Orasha mountain. They felt a sense of loss and loneliness as they watched Lembarta, Lenjirr and Masintet walking down the path that led them back to their village. The rest of the crowd of villagers that had come out to escort them, had already bid them farewell and returned back to their village. Masintet turned and waved. Norpisia returned his wave, tears welling up in her eyes, she was suddenly overcome by the knowledge that she might never see the people of Eorr-Narasha again. In the short time she had known them, she had come to love them. They had welcomed her, accepted her as one of their own, and had asked her to live with them. Had it been possible, she could have accepted.

Kedoki felt desolate as well, watching his friend Masintet and his two brothers turning back toward their home. He recalled that Masintet and Lembarta saved his life and Norpisia's and their livestock, not once, but several times, during that treacherous journey through the wilderness. Although he gave each one of them ten heifers, he felt he could never have rewarded them sufficiently for their valour and selflessness. Only *Enkai-Narok* could reward them by showering them with his mercy and blessings.

They drove their animals toward the west across the savannah. Their four tamed wildebeests were still in their herd. Not long after, they came upon the valley in which a smaller river flowed eastward on its way to the bigger Ilkarian river. The valley was broad, with a gentle grassy slope and the livestock grazed on it contentedly for sometime.

Suddenly, the only remaining dog dashed away, barking. It had sniffed the scent of an animal which turned out to be an eland. The dog ran to it barking fiercely. But when the stag lowered its head to fend off the charging dog, it halted. Kedoki noticed that the magnificent long horns of the powerful animal were each three feet long! The great beast nibbled on the grass paying little attention to the dog.

Norpisia smiled as she watched the timid dog. "Look at the dog," she said chuckling, "It thought the eland was another goat it could pester!"

"It got surprised at the length of those sharp horns," Kedoki said smiling.

"The length of those horns is a lot longer than I expected to see on an eland," Norpisia commented. "Come to think of it, I have never been this close to one before."

During the conversation, Norpisia noticed that Kedoki seemed absent-minded. For the last seven days since they came to Eorr-Narasha, he seemed distracted and had the look of anxious concern.

"*Olpayian lai,*" she called him fondly. "Do you remember one time when you were angry with me because I did not tell you what was bothering me?"

He had been so deeply immersed in his thoughts that it took a few seconds before he comprehended her question.

"Of course I do remember," he answered wondering what was in her mind. "Then you were wondering whether I loved you. I hope you are still not in doubt."

"No, I don't have any doubts about that," she said emphatically. "I have noticed that of late, something is constantly bothering you. What is it?"

"I am worried about crossing the Ilkarian river," he said in a serious voice. "It is treacherous and during the rainy seasons like now, it becomes too dangerous to cross."

"Well, if it is too dangerous to cross, then we won't attempt to cross it."

"Do you know what that means? It means, we shall not get to our home," he said lightheartedly. "Then we shall have Norpisia to thank for our failure to go home. Do you know why? She is the cause of all this rain. It is said, and I have no doubt it is true, that the trees you helped to plant have resuscitated the environment, and the resuscitated environment has brought the rain, and the rains have flooded Ilkarian river. The result? Kedoki and his beloved Norpisia cannot get to their home at Nkararo."

Norpisia roared with rich uproarious laughter. Too much of a good thing cannot be bad, she told herself happily. The rains were no exception.

"If we can't cross Ilkarian river," she asked still laughing, "what do we do next? We ought to go back and establish our permanent homestead at Eorr-Narasha."

Kedoki did not answer. A revived determination to cross the river seized him. There was nothing he longed for more than to settle Norpisia in his own homestead, and in his own village at Nkararo.

He decided that they should cross the river, immediately! So, he walked her down to survey the Ilkarian river that was not far. The river was deep and the current swift, and the large jagged boulders created rapids in various places. They checked the condition both upstream and downstream, and the nature of the river seemed consistent from a distance. Finally, they selected a section that seemed relatively free of rocks and safe. They chose that afternoon as the ideal time for crossing, after ascertaining that the level of the water in the river had not increased as a result of flooding upstream.

Kedoki watched Norpisia express her bewilderment with the surrounding. Her beauty was accentuated by her sparkling eyes and her beautiful smile. What a beautiful wife he had in Norpisia!

Although he enjoyed seeing beautiful scenes like the one before them, he knew his own enthusiasm for the dramatic panorama was fired by her sheer excitement.

And it was always in such moments that he watched her express her appreciation of nature's beauty excitedly. It could have been jealousy, or selfishness on his part, but he knew that part of the reason why he wanted to take her away to Nkararo was to allow himself spend more time with her. There were too many external forces at Eorr-Narasha that constantly pulled her away from him. Women friends such as Ngoto Lesiamin would not give them a moment to be alone. And when Sein, the prophetess came, she monopolized her, keeping her away from him for hours on end. A wife's first priority was her husband, he reasoned and declared that such other mundane things like leading women to resuscitate the environment, sitting by the fire for long hours boiling herbal concoctions to treat hordes of sick people, were all secondary. Now that he was taking her to Nkararo, that beloved place where he belonged, Norpisia's love would no longer be shared with other people.

"Yes, so beautiful and so exciting," he said finally.

Something in his voice sent a shiver through her and made her turn to look at him closely. She saw a look of love and adoration in his eyes. She blinked with tears. He was unable to look directly at her and pulled away to looked down the river.

"*Norpisia-ai nanyorr,*" he called her adoringly. "Do you have any idea how much I love you?"

She knew it was true that he loved her. She had always known it and saw it in his eyes. Yes, she had always seen it in his brilliant, vivid, black eyes that caressed her with their look. His eyes always expressed the emotions that his cultural sensibilities could not allow him to show, and he tried so hard to keep them under control.

"I know that you love me dearly, my husband," she said quietly. "And I know you know that I also love you beyond words."

Kedoki scrutinized her, loving the sight of her full womanly form, and delighting in the knowledge that she belonged to him entirely. As they stood at the top of the scenic hill, his shadow fell across her, blocking the heat of the sun. Norpisia opened her eyes and looked up and she saw the brilliant sun behind him, giving his shadowed face a golden aura.

"The sooner we cross this river," Kedoki said staring intently at the valley below, "the better it would be for us and our animals."

Norpisia stepped out of the shadows and walked beside her husband as they moved downhill. Kedoki shifted Kinyamal from one shoulder to the other.

They both continued to walk down the hill and drove the animals fast toward the river. They watched the movement of the water as it swiftly flowed downstream. The banks were overflowing and they could see logs, trees and other debris floating, bobbing and dipping as the agitated water ebbed and flowed over the riverside.

"We have to drive the livestock quickly through the water, otherwise they may become stubborn," Kedoki said as he ran up and down whipping the cattle into one group. "Let us not allow them to scatter."

The cattle suddenly became stubborn and obstinately refused to get into the water however hard they prodded at them with their sticks. There was total confusion as their herd scattered and ran into all directions. Kedoki ran hastily, his son still perched on his shoulders as he shouted at the wayward animals trying to regroup them. Norpisia also moved from one direction to the other hitting the stubborn animals hard with her stick trying to push them into the water. Then she suddenly saw her four wildebeests race up the hill followed by the donkey that carried their personal effects.

At that moment, there was a resounding roar of thunder, the sky opened and was lit by a sudden shaft of lightning. Norpisia jerked with shock and shivered with dread as bright flashes illuminated the hills behind them. But it was not the lightning that scared her: She dreaded the explosive sound it presaged. She recoiled each time she heard a distant rumble or a nearby rolling boom. Each burst of thunder shook more rain down harder. Then what they feared most suddenly happened: something that must have been blocking the river upstream, suddenly gave way and great volumes of water gushed downstream with such speed and force that nothing could have stood on its way. All their cattle, sheep and goats were at once swept away together with the elephants, buffaloes and other animals that had been swept from the highlands and carried downstream. When Kedoki turned to look at the place where Norpisia had been, she was not there. His heart went cold with fright.

"Norpisia! Norpisia! Where are you?" he called. There was no answer. He called out again and again but there was no answer. In the midst of moving objects, all he could see were reeds. In a sudden panic, he called out again as he confusedly ran up and down in the water with Kinyamal who was still perched on his shoulders.

"Norpisia! Norpisia! Where in the name of God can you be?"

What took place happened so fast that Norpisia had no time to think. Water suddenly rose to the level above her knees, and it was propelled by a strong current. She began to move back, edging toward the dry ground. Then the ground abruptly disappeared as her feet were swept from under her, and her scream was a thin wail, lost in the rumbling sound of the flooded river. Utter panic possessed her mind as the water enveloped her and filled her mouth and nose. She began to spin as she was being swept rapidly along, and tumbled as cold water crushed in around her. She struggled frantically, fighting to get her head out of the water. She raised her head and gulped deep breaths as she struggled to pull herself out of the water. She dimly saw a large object floating by her and she dragged herself toward it. It turned out to be one of their drowned cows. It slipped and slid sideways as she tried to climb onto it, but in the process, one of her feet found a firm tree. She pulled herself higher and began to climb, chocking and vomiting water she had swallowed. It was then that she heard Kedoki's voice calling her. She clung to the tree she was perched on as the rain continued to pound on her relentlessly. All around her was the gushing roar of the swollen river. She inched her way along the trunk of the tree, coughing, chocking and gasping for air. Her *lesos* were torn into shreds, having been caught by twigs and brush and she had to forcefully pull them loose out of their clutches. All around her, she saw many of their drowned cows and many wild animals wedged firmly between trees to where they had been pushed by the raging flood water. She listened again and to her consternation, she heard more than one voice calling out her name. Was she a victim of hallucination? She wondered whether she was dreaming. The voices reached her again, and that time round they were clear and sounded familiar. She could hear Kedoki's voice and that of Lembarta and Masintet. And incredibly still, she heard the voice of Eddah Sein the prophetess. Was that possible? She wondered.

Then suddenly, something stirred on the edge of her awareness, tugging at her attention. Her mind began to slowly draw out of her reverie and like one waking up from deep slumber, she began to realize where she was and comprehend what had happened. She saw four large dark shadows moving toward her in the rain. The rain still fell on her face as she lifted it to scrutinize the blurred outline of the three well-known and familiar faces of Lembarta, Masintet and Sein. Carrying her son on his shoulders was her husband, Kedoki. They all rushed to her and Sein bent over her, took her arms and lifted her. The men helped her to carry Norpisia to the vehicle, where she wrapped her in a warm *leso*. Kedoki sat next to her, still shocked by the hellish experience they had just undergone, but exultant that although he had lost all his cattle, sheep and goats, Norpisia was safe.

Soon, they were on their way to Nakuru through the green dense forest that Norpisia had helped to establish.